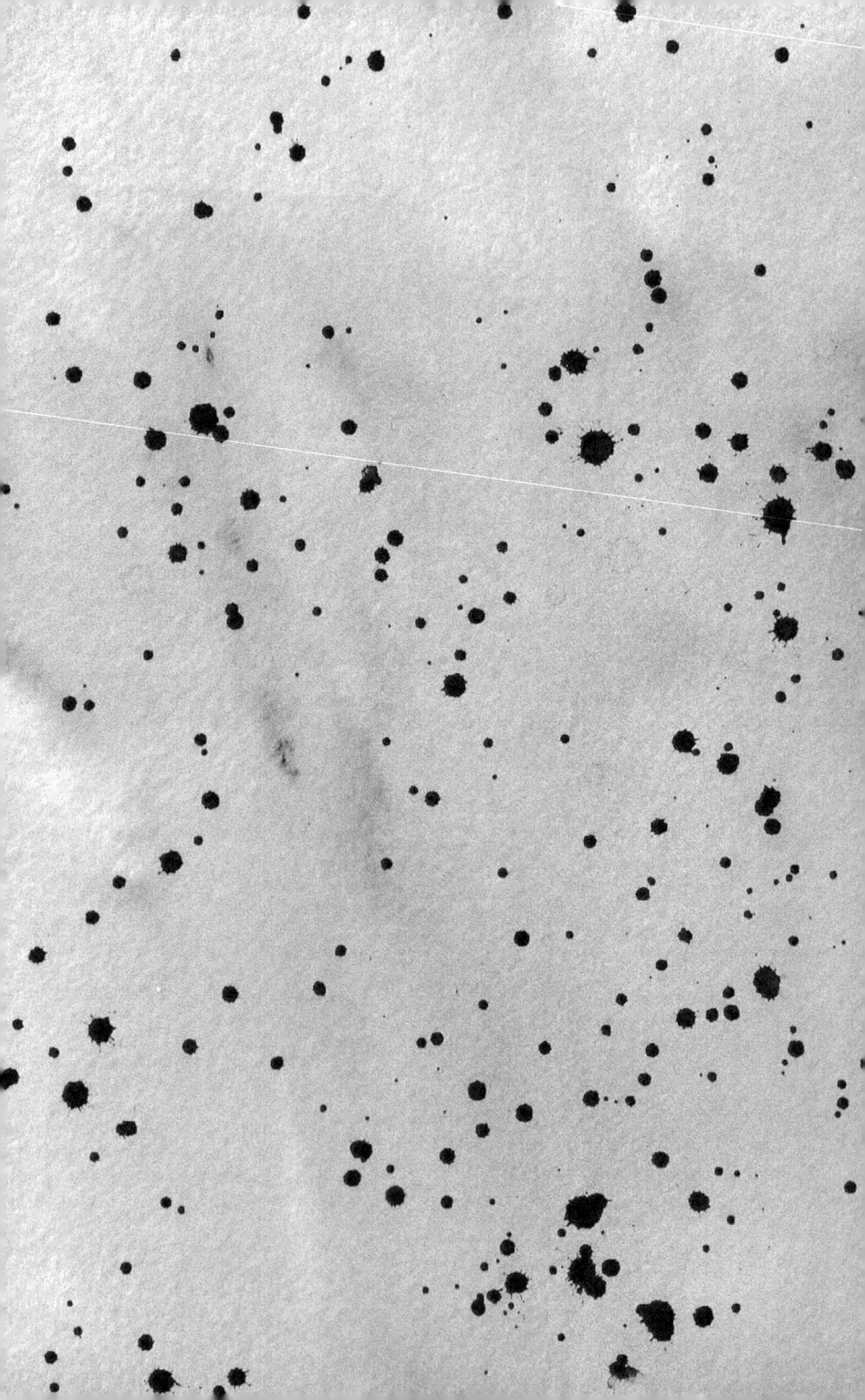

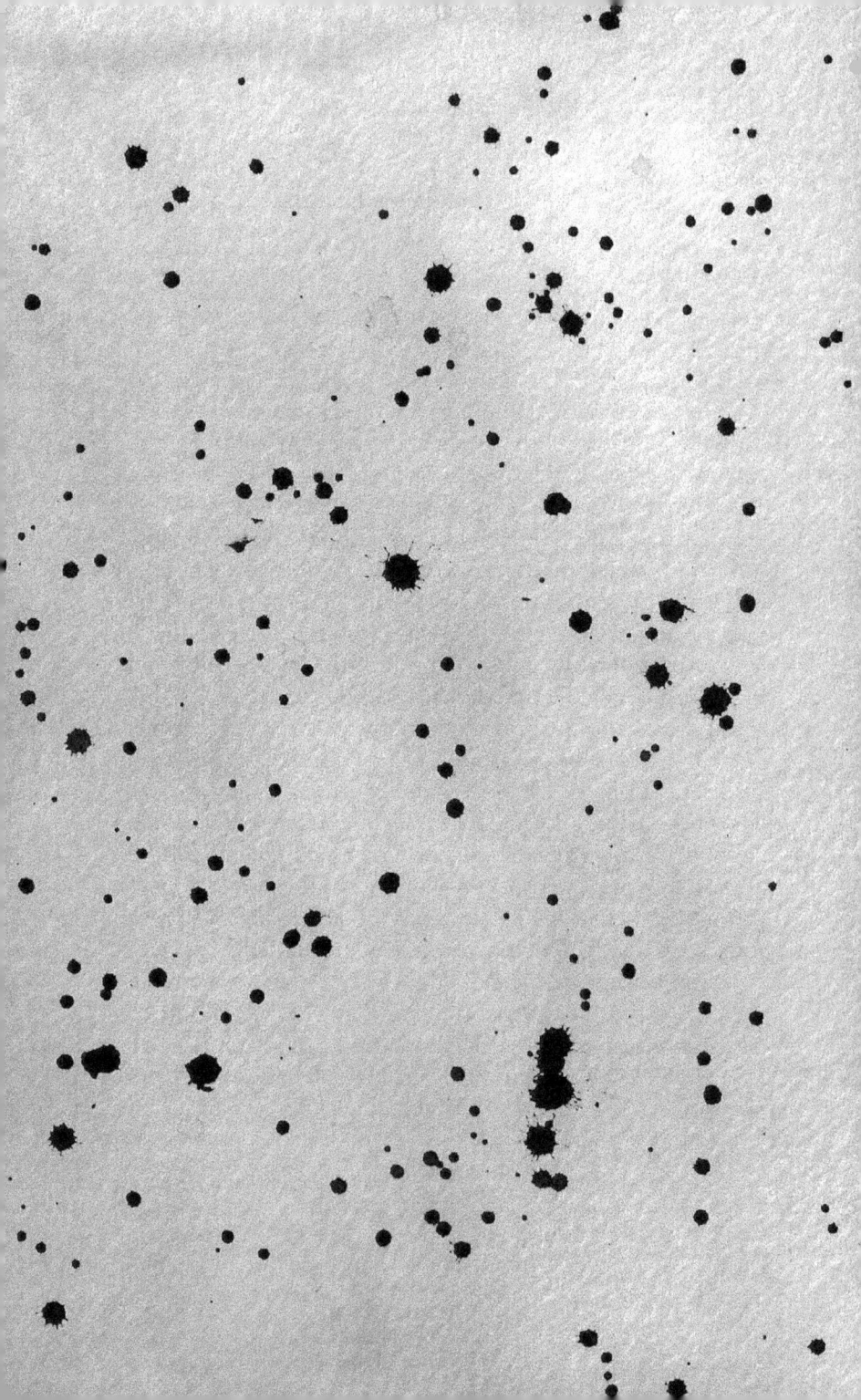

WHAT THE CRITICS ARE SAYING ABOUT
The $22.50 Man
Book Two of the Genji Trilogy

In this comic Depression-era sequel, two newlyweds flee underworld connections to start a new life. Jean-Yves LeFouet has a way of getting into trouble not of his own making. Having left New York City in 1929 for California to avoid repercussions from his shady boss's downfall, he must make a return trip. Apparently, the copies of *The Tale of Genji*, a 1,000-year-old Japanese novel that he was ferrying to actors he thought would be auditioning for a film version, actually contained heroin, and the law got after him. It's now 1935, and Jean-Yves wants to go straight; he's newly married to Ariane (part Japanese, part French), his perfect match: "We're made for each other. We love poetry and film and theater and one another." When the cops come knocking, the couple (and their cat, Vince) manage to escape to the Big Apple. Ariane finds work in a bookstore while Jean-Yves, who has exceptionally sharp hearing, is offered an informant job with the New York City Police Department for which he'll drive a taxi, eavesdrop on fares, and collect $22.50 a week. Typically, Jean-Yves—now calling himself John Still—nabs customs scofflaws, but soon he has a bigger target in Jacob Racker, a tannery owner and supplier of shoe leather to the NYPD. When Asian rubber-sole makers threaten to undercut him, Racker is willing to bribe political bigwigs. Meanwhile, John writes a story based on his life, and Ariane translates a Japanese woman's ancient scroll of poetry (found in a cocktail shaker), then writes and films a play based on it. After losing his $22.50 a week job, John is hired to drive a truck for Racker's tannery, where he becomes involved in solving a crime—and gets back into trouble.

As the author did in the first book of this trilogy, *Shooting Genji* (2014), Voorhees conjures up his historical period with slangy high spirits appropriate to the Jazz Age setting. The fast-moving plot packs a lot of action and well-honed characterizations into these pages, as when Otis—Racker's nephew with a goldbricking, low-level job at the tannery—defends his status: "We're like chemists."

But the author is a storytelling master who has many registers available to him, from a cat's point of view ("Hide hide. Under the room-that-goes. I'm big. Don't come. I'm big") to the scroll's heartbroken poet, whose work is extremely touching in Ariane's translations: "If you pick up a faded bouquet gently, / And try to toss it away, / The petals will fall off / on the floor / at your feet. / It's the same with you and me." A subplot involving Racker's maid and a poker-playing fellow taxi driver hooks up with the main story nicely in ways both amusing and tender. It's a short book and over all too quickly; fans will be eager for the trilogy's final volume. Voorhees' monochrome watercolor illustrations deftly accompany the text, recalling Japanese ink-brush paintings with an extra splash-dab of verve.

A wonderfuly appealing, literate, compassionate, and funny Jazz Age tale; a home run!

—*Kirkus Reviews*

THE $22.50 MAN

Other Works by Richard Voorhees

Shooting Genji (novel)
(Book One of the Genji Trilogy)

A Little Too Rambunctious (novel)

The Royal and Ancient Golf Curse (novel)

Old Pros (A Literary Dictionary of the World's Oldest Professions)

Proust + Vermeer (film)

Mr. Cool's How Not-To Guide (film)

Be-Bop-A-Lula (screenplay)

Strummer in the City (screenplay)

Props (screenplay)

The Roll Call of Ghosts (play)

THE $22.50 MAN

WRITTEN AND ILLUSTRATED BY
RICHARD VOORHEES

Book Two of the Genji Trilogy

Found Art Publishing
Seattle, Washington

The $22.50 Man. Copyright © 2020 Richard Voorhees.
All rights reserved. Printed in the United States of America.
No part of this book may be used or reproduced in any manner
without prior written permission, except in the case of brief
quotations embodied in critical articles and reviews.

The $22.50 Man is a work of fiction. Any resemblance to persons
living or dead is coincidental and unintended.

No part of this book may be used as data for 'training' any large
language model or as part of any machine learning or neural
network architecture.

Front cover illustration: Richard Voorhees
Book design by JM Shubin, BookAlchemist.net
and Tim Braun, timbraundesign.myportfolio.com

CATALOGING DATA:
Voorhees, Richard.
    The $22.50 Man / Richard Voorhees.
    p. cm.
    ISBN 978-1-966297-00-0

Publisher's Cataloging-in-Publication Data

Names: Voorhees, Richard, author.
Title: The 22.50 man / written and illustrated by Richard Voorhees.
Series: The Genji Trilogy.
Description: Seattle, WA: Found Art Publishing, 2025.
Identifiers: ISBN 978-1-966297-00-0
Subjects: LCSH Taxicab drivers--New York (State)--New York--Fiction. |
Informers--New York (State)--New York--Fiction. | New York (N.Y.)--
History--Fiction.| Criminal investigation--Fiction. | Japan--History--
Heian period, 794-1185--Fiction. | Man-woman relationships--Fiction. |
Noir fiction. | Mystery fiction. | Historical fiction. | BISAC FICTION /
Noir | FICTION / Mystery & Detective / Historical
Classification: LCC PS3622.O695 T9 2025 | DDC 813.6--dc23

Second Edition

To Pammy

Dictionary of American Underworld Lingo:

"TWENTY-TWO-FIFTY MEN."
(New York City; Obsolete).

Informers. A term applied to taxicab drivers, and other people regarded as assistant policemen.

[Note: In the early 1920's the N.Y. City police department is alleged to have retained the services of such aides at a weekly salary of $22.50. Most of them were awaiting examination for positions in the police department. The term endures, although the conditions that gave rise to it are all but forgotten.]

Editors: Hyman E. Goldin, Frank O'Leary, and Morris Lipsius. Twayne Publishers, Inc. (1950).

CONTENTS

A Purramble	1
Chapter 1: A Knock at the Door	3
Chapter 2: Running Back East	10
Chapter 3: Off Broadway	16
Chapter 4: By the Sound of It	19
Chapter 5: Gourmet Fare	25
Chapter 6: Flea Market	30
Chapter 7: Listening In	33
Chapter 8: A Dented Cocktail Shaker	37
Chapter 9: The Creek that Sang	42
Chapter 10: My Thoughts Are a Snowstorm	44
Chapter 11: The Crash of 1935	47
Chapter 12: Kitchen War	49
Chapter 13: Fashioning a Goblet of Hemlock	55
Chapter 14: The Paradox of the Intimate	58
Chapter 15: A Whale Washes Ashore	62
Chapter 16: 52-Card Pickup	64
Chapter 17: Getting Dizzy	66
Chapter 18: Salt Grinder	69
Chapter 19: The Mayor	76
Chapter 20: Talk of Shoes	79
Chapter 21: Flat-Footed	81
Chapter 22: Lotta Trouble	86
Chapter 23: Be Forewarned	88
Chapter 24: Traveling in Style	90
Chapter 25: A Shambles	96

Chapter 26: New York Steak	98
Chapter 27: Some Mug	100
Chapter 28: Caught in Flagrante Delicto	102
Chapter 29: Lotta Explaining	108
Chapter 30: A Prince	116
Chapter 31: The Poet's Dream	119
Chapter 32: 1,000 Years Ago, in Japan	122
Chapter 33: At Large	131
Chapter 34: The Bum's Rush	136
Chapter 35: Golf Cart Surveillance	138
Chapter 36: Furrier and Furrier	141
Chapter 37: Graveyard Shift	148
Chapter 38: Cat Napping	152
Chapter 39: Turpitude	154
Chapter 40: Those Who Feed	156
Chapter 41: Death in the Tannery	159
Chapter 42: Interrogation	162
Chapter 43: Tap of the Morning	166
Chapter 44: Lotta Fun	170
Chapter 45: Deadpan Dora	172
Chapter 46: A Comedy of Errors	175
Chapter 47: Dredging Up the Past	178
Chapter 48: Bad Dog	181
Chapter 49: The Coroner Studies the Classics	185
Chapter 50: Cat Hill	188
Chapter 51: Filing My Final Report	189
Chapter 52: A Circle within a Circle	192

ILLUSTRATIONS

A Sometime Actress	xvi
John Still	xvii
Vince Takes Cover	xviii
An Ill Wind Blows No Good	6
Starry Night	12
"We Want You…"	22
The Dragon and the Lotus	32
Sweltering Night in Brooklyn	35
The Wordless Haiku	60
Flat Feet	84
Mister Customs Man	95
Invasion of Privacy	104
The Salt Burner's Daughter	120
Staging Genji	126
Central Park After Dark	136
The Room-That-Goes	142
Follow That Cat	158
Vince on Ice	169
Bad Dog	182

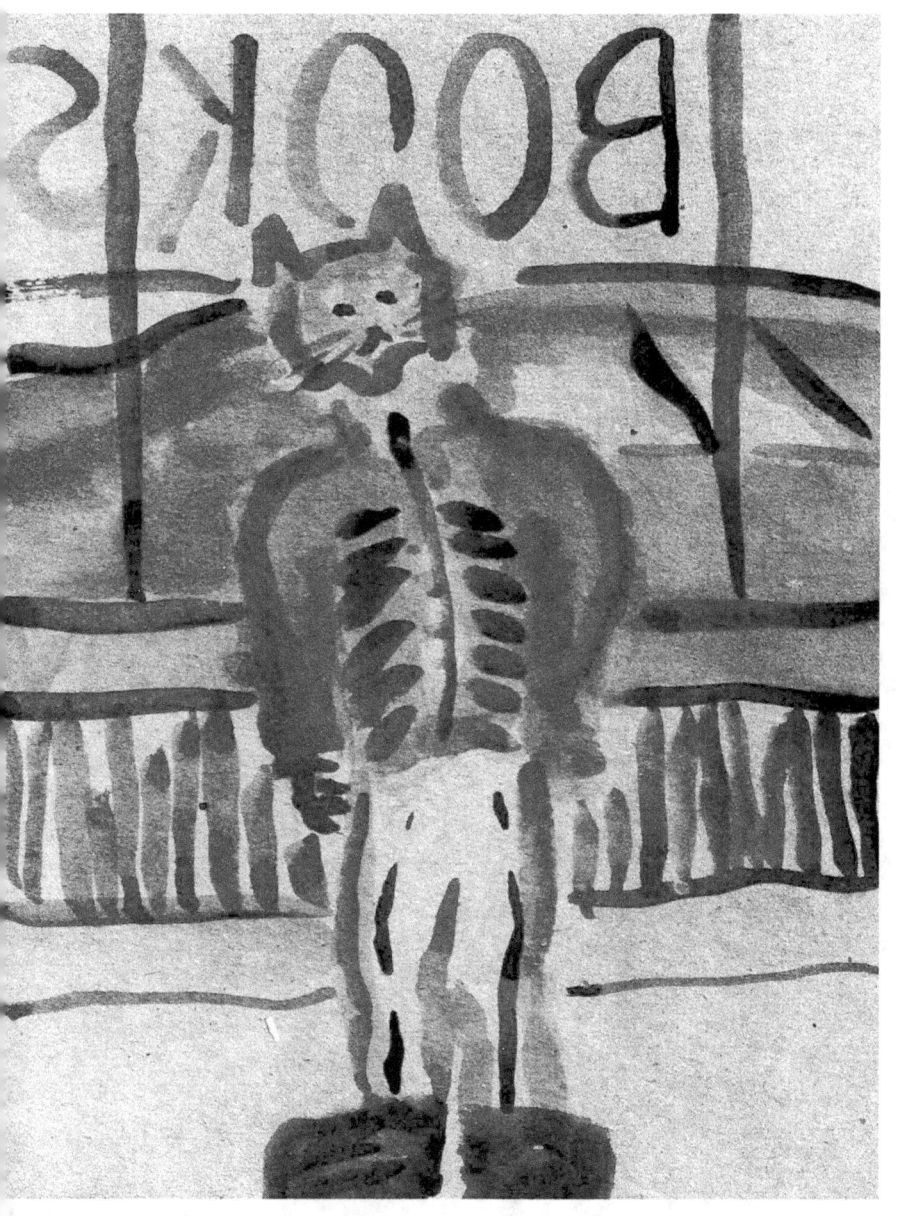

Richard Voorhees

A PURRAMBLE

What the bang? Ssssss… cat! Fly flee run scratchy screaming fly. Hide hide. Under the room-that-goes. I'm big. Don't come. I'm big. You can't see me in the dark. Crouch. I see big cats. I see paws many paws. Flat paws. What are they carrying? Why are they dropping it? Why are they unrolling it?

Oh! There's a really really really big cat lying on it. He looks hurt. One big cat pulls a loud banging clanging thing out of the ground. Then all the big cats rush and grab the big hurt cat and they pick it up. They make all sorts of meows trying to move the sick cat. They put the sick cat's head into a hole in the ground. They lift him up by the hind legs and he sticks there, head in the ground, legs in the air. He's too big. They say meow like they mean it.

Then I hear him fall and make a sound like the big wet. Shoosh. They shove the clanging thing back in the ground. Then they run here at me! They all scramble in the room-that-goes and I hear the roar and I screech out away away. The room-that-goes ssssss at me as it moves fast. It snarls away. That smell I don't like. It smells like big cats that hurry. Big cats are dangerous when they're in a hurry.

CHAPTER 1

A KNOCK AT THE DOOR
Los Angeles – 1935

On our wedding night, when we turn out the lights, I've forgotten about everything except how beautiful Ariane is, how the sight of her makes me catch my breath, how she's oxygen for a man suffocating on beauty.

Trust me, I know what it means to draw your last breath. Why, just the other day, Big Department—head honcho of the Green Gang—was throttling Akihiro and me, one in each hand. That's when that broker Squidrow came to our rescue and shot him. It wasn't easy ditching his carcass down that manhole. What a behemoth. He made a splash like Lulu in Hollywood.

We'd convinced Big Department to short rubber companies, tire companies, and golf ball manufacturers, telling him that synthetic rubber was going to be the next big thing.

Regrettably, the price of rubber soared anyway, despite our best efforts, because of talk of war in Europe. Squidrow was only trying to collect on our losing short bets when he sprang into action, put a bullet in Big Department, and stopped him cold.

All because of one little investment. I would have thought the huge Brit was one of those high-net-worth characters who can afford a bad bet. Big Department had heard enough. He wanted to shut our mouths for good like that manhole cover.

We considered telling the cops, pointing out we were the wronged parties. But just knowing the "gentleman from Shanghai" put you at a disadvantage vis-à-vis the LAPD. It might have led them straight to those copies of *The Tale of Genji* that I unwittingly delivered all over L.A.

I counseled against running into the arms of the law. Big Department got what was coming to him. No one was going to miss him. The cops might even be on his payroll, and their meal ticket had just been torn to pieces. Maybe we could play it cool, keep on like nothing cataclysmic had happened.

Ariane's grandmother summoned Japanese exorcists to cleanse the karmic residue of violence and death from her bookstore, the Dragon and the Lotus.

One evening Ariane's grandmother gave a reading of some of her translation of *The Tale of Genji* to a gathering of neighbors in Little Tokio. She wanted to consecrate her bookstore anew. Then welcome silence ensued, and we began to think we'd slid out from under the big gangster's shadow.

That's when we decide to elope. We're made for each other. We love poetry and film and theater and one another. I'm trying to go straight and Ariane's my better angel.

But, alas, late one night not long after there's a knock at the door, and it's loud. Somber and authoritative, like a cop playing a requiem on a bass drum. Bam bam bam. Bam.

I go for my gun under the bed and slide out, motioning to Ariane to get down. As quietly as I can, I creep over to the window, trying not to bump into the furniture. Through a gap in the curtains, I see it's not the cops. It's that huge lug, my old acquaintance, Poochie, and that Irish sailor, the one who looks like a barracuda. How they found us, I've no idea. The Hudson is parked around the corner. That probably tipped them off. They staked out the place and I turned up.

Last time I saw Poochie was on the beach of a tiny cove, just before he cold-cocked me and left me free to drown in the dark in a rising tide. He and his pal were shoving off in a stolen yacht.

The force of that blow straightened out my eyesight for a few days, or maybe it was the impact the ground made when I lay me down. That's to say, I was no longer overly sensitive to sunlight or moonlight. At the same time, I've come to realize my hearing's gotten sharper. My ears rang for a couple days after Poochie slugged me, but when that went away, I started hearing tiny sounds I'd never noticed before. There's more friction in the world than I realized. And as things rub up against one another, I hear it. Even a breath of wind in the trees.

To say I'm in no hurry to talk to these two is an understatement. I wait, gun in hand, crouched in the dark,

Richard Voorhees

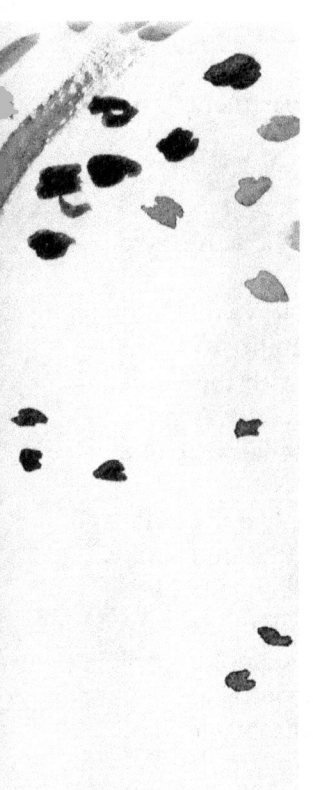

hoping they don't make a night of using my door for a drum. Ariane's bravely covering me, pointing her Derringer at the front door. It sounds like it's about to crack. We're a couple of real desperadoes, or if we weren't before, we are now.

Poochie tries turning the knob quietly. Thank God, I'd locked it. (You never know.) Then he gives it a more determined wrench. You can get a sick feeling seeing a doorknob twisted hard like that. I wouldn't put it past him to twist the doorknob completely off and bust on in. There's not nearly enough wall between us if they start shooting.

They're talking, muffled. Then comes Poochie's voice, deep and laconic: "Open up, Stilly, if you know what's good for you."

I guess I don't. Or I have other ideas on the subject of what's good for me. He twists the doorknob a last couple times, as if he's strangling it. A vicious kick to the door makes the whole house jump. Bad for the nerves, but the door hangs on to its hinges.

All falls silent. Then I hear an engine start up and a car peel out.

"Bad news," I say, shaking my head without really even realizing it. "Evidently."

"Who was that?"

"Guys who used to work for Big Department. The ones who left me for dead."

"Oh, no."

"We have to get out of here."

"We don't have much," says Ariane. "I won't take long."

We put a light on in the bathroom and leave the door slightly ajar. When I still had an uncanny ability to see in the dark, we could have packed our bags with the lights out. Thanks to my falling for Manon. Literally. A crack on the head. But no longer. I'm like a pinball machine on tilt.

It's true Ariane and I don't have much… we're newlyweds… some sky-blue satiny numbers… the Hudson… a little money stashed in the pages of *The Tale of Genji*… some other treasured books… my notebook of ideas for the tale I'm scratching out… Ariane's notebook full of poems… some food in the icebox… some outtakes.

How'd Poochie pick up my trail? The last time I saw him and Finnbar, they were sailing away toward destinations undisclosed. The L.A. police had given them twenty-four hours to leave town and never come back. They should be in Shanghai. Where East does meet West. Or Puerto Vallarta. Where orange and lime meet tequila. Not yelling at our door. If anyone's leaving no forwarding address, it's us.

"Ready?"

"I think so."

"All right, my beauty, let's go."

"What about the kitty cat?"

"Right, Vince!"

All that banging spooked Vince, and he's still lying low. We find him and coax him out from under the dresser. With suitcases in hand and the cat firmly clamped in the crook of my arm, we slip out of our itty-bitty apartment and hurry around the corner to the Hudson. Vince is digging his claws into me, trying to get away. But I've got a good hold of him, and we shove our earthly goods into the back seat then spring into the car together. I nick my ankle with the car door as I jump in beside Ariane. We race out of there, hoping no one's crouching or lurking.

I know how to get out of town quick. Make like the Santa Anas and blow.

I would give you a more detailed description of us… if we weren't on the lam. I know I mentioned in the first installment of our story, *Shooting Genji*, that I'm pretty tall and that Ariane is part-Japanese and part-French. But I don't want the people who are after us to have more dope to go on than that. Thank you for respecting my privacy. I did say that Ariane looks something like Louise Brooks. I look like a reflection in a window at night.

CHAPTER 2

RUNNING BACK EAST

I feel the boat slowing and the sea calming. I hear a door shut and someone fiddling with the trap. The hatch opens and it's dark out. My eyes are blurry, but I make out Ariane, looking in on me, smiling slightly, concerned.

"Am I dreaming?"

"No, no. You're waking up. Come. Give me your arm. Sit up slowly."

"Ooo, ooo, oof."

"Take your time. It's all right."

"Where am I?"

"In the middle of nowhere."

"With you?"

"Yes, with me."

"Are you sure I'm not dreaming?"

I sit up and see I'm not in a boat after all. I'm in the back seat of a land yacht. The Hudson. It's coming back to me.

My neck and shoulders are locked up as if I were some failed, second-rate contortionist. I manage to unfold out of the car, and slowly, very slowly reach for the sky. There are a million stars overhead and desert all around. We're either in Death Valley or on the moon.

"When you feel up to it, you drive the next stretch?"

"Of course!"

"You've been asleep for quite a while. As you can see, the sun's quite down. I'm exhausted."

"Give me a couple seconds. The back seat's not as roomy as it looks."

"Sorry."

"I had a terrible dream."

"What was it about?"

"I dreamt I'd been shanghaied. That I was locked in the hold of a ship and a thousand miles at sea. I've had it before."

"You can tell me all about it while you drive. This car's better suited for someone tall. My feet are tired stretching to reach the pedals."

I gyrate some more, rub my eyes, and look again at the heavens.

"Have you ever seen so many stars?"

"On a moonless night on the Pacific, fleeing Shanghai for America," Ariane admits.

"Do you want to try to sleep in back?"

"I'd rather keep you company."

"All right, sweetheart, hop in. Where are we anyway?"

"Somewhere in Nevada. While you were sleeping, I kept thinking about my grandmother and the bookstore

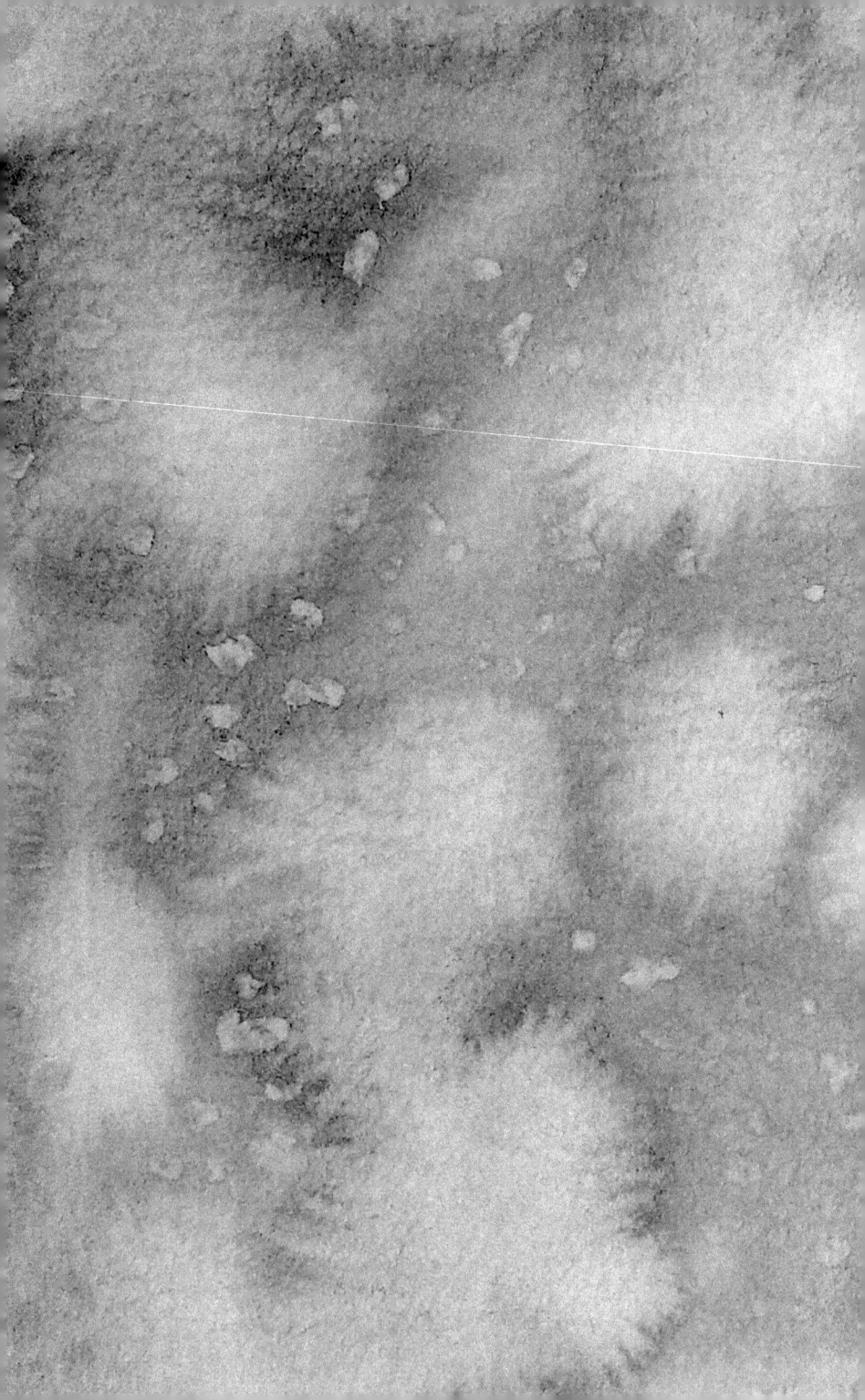

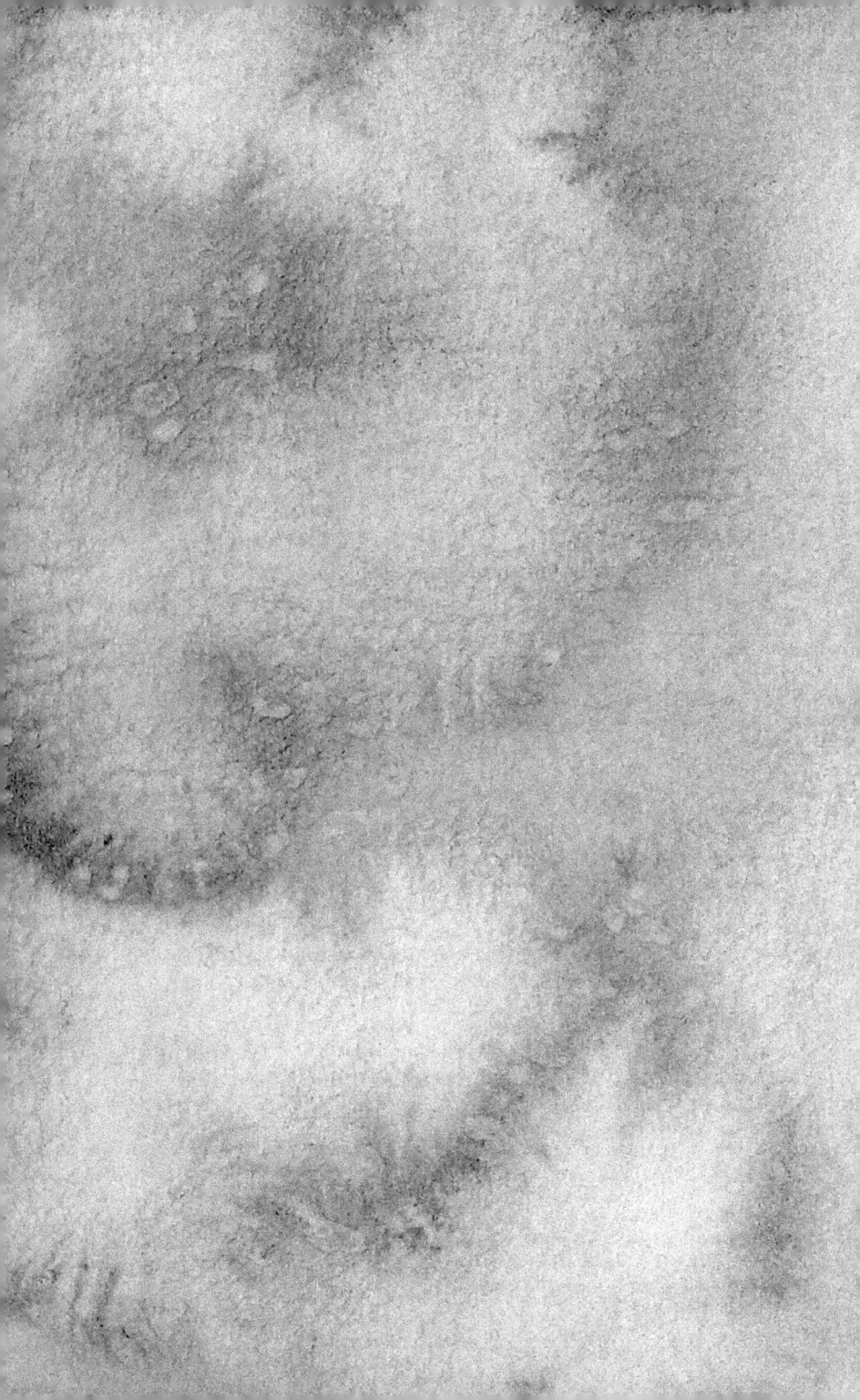

and my rooftop garden. I'm really worried. I love you, Jean-Yves, but my life, so much is back there."

"I'm sorry, Ariane, truly."

"Who will water my jasmine?"

"Your grandmother?" I suggest idiotically.

"Can you imagine her trying to climb the ladder to the roof? If she made it up there, she'd be paralyzed. Like a cat in a plum tree," Ariane murmurs.

"Or a car with no reverse."

"Exactly," she says. "Life is like that: a cat climbing higher and higher in a plum tree. A car with no reverse."

"It would be insane to stay in L.A.," I say.

"It's her bookstore. She's very strong, really, if she uses her cane. And tough-minded. You've seen her."

"She's got that gun. Didn't she say she'd heard from your uncle, Akihiro, that he said something about helping her? He's a ladder climber. He can water your garden and sell books."

"He'll probably just use the Dragon and the Lotus as a front."

"He's a tricky guy, but I trust him myself."

"I do, too," says Ariane.

"We'll visit bookstores all across America."

"Of course, we will. And across Canada. Your family's in Montreal, aren't they? I've always wanted to see Canada. I want to meet your parents."

"I want them to meet you, Ariane, darling. But I can't go back to Canada. I'd be walking into trouble."

"Oh!" says Ariane, clearly disappointed and a little taken aback.

"Maybe someday."

"I'm sorry."

"Meantime, maybe we can start collecting inventory for a new bookstore," I say, trying to stay positive.

"I'd like that."

"We'll plant you a new rooftop garden."

"It's a must. Do you really think I'll like New York?"

"I hope so. It's full of book readers. And there's Broadway."

"The real theater," she says.

"Uh-huh."

"Hmm. That's funny," Ariane exclaims. "I thought we were planning on having an uneventful life!"

"What do plans have to do with life?"

"They often go awry," Ariane says softly.

"Such a small word, 'life.' It should be spelled 't-o-r-n-a-d-o.'"

"Ours, here, right now, is Nevada. N-e-v-a-d-a. The Nevada desert at three in the morning," Ariane replies, yawning.

"So many stars," I say, looking out the window. I turn the key in the ignition. "We have each other, and, uh… it looks like about a quarter tank of gas."

CHAPTER 3

OFF BROADWAY
Lower Manhattan – 1935

When we get to New York City, Ariane and I find a sublet on the Lower East Side that we can afford, advertised on a typed card on a bulletin board in a hole-in-the-wall bookstore on St. Marks. We waste no time. It's only a few blocks away and a couple minutes later we're climbing the steep front steps of a brownstone on 3rd Street, between Avenues A and B. The heavy outside door's unlocked, so I hold it for Ariane and we walk down a dim corridor to the apartment listed on the card. It's actually the neighbor's place. The old guy is home and he takes us next door to see the apartment that's for rent. He waits while we look around.

It's a pretty typical New York apartment—a little living room, a couple small bedrooms, a tiny bathroom that's attached to a tiny kitchen. Steam heat. The pipes clank and bang randomly. The most startling thing about the place, though, is the dust. A book duster's nemesis. It reminds me of some ancient Egyptian tomb. The apartment is furnished, but everything is buried in a half-inch of dust. It's so thick and heavy in places it's practically topsoil.

"I take it no one's lived here in a while?"

"That's right. The owner's been away, and she just found out she's going to be away a lot longer than she thought."

"What does she do?"

"She's a professor."

"Of what?"

"Archeology."

"Ahh. She must feel right at home here."

"What do you think, Ariane?"

"I like the light."

"I do, too."

"And the neighborhood."

"Yeah."

"It could use a thorough cleaning."

"For sure. Or excavating."

The neighbor says he can lend us a broom and a mop and a bucket. We're pretty wrung out ourselves after driving cross-country from L.A. We can rent it a month at a time. It's cheap. Okay, we decide to take it. We get busy with our own archeological dig and a couple days later the place looks a million times better. The light filtering through the trees outside the windows in the afternoon is especially nice. Now that we have a base, we start thinking about finding some gainful employ. Ariane begins talking to bookstore owners, one after the other, and I start looking for work driving or working back on Wall Street or in a film lab, or maybe if I'm lucky, working on a film production. I see a job posted for a sound editor and go apply.

CHAPTER 4

BY THE SOUND OF IT

I find the address and the place is a big warehouse of a building in Times Square. It's a warren inside, full of small rooms where guys are intently hunched over film splicers editing films. All that film coiling out of those editing machines reminds me of L.A. and working on our misbegotten film of *The Tale of Genji*. All that work and it only got shown once. Those lassoes of film also remind me of some poor guy in the hospital whose guts are spilling out.

I poke my head in the room where they're advertising for a sound editor and it's a completely different setup. It's filled with microphones, tape recorders, electrical cables, and editing equipment. I haven't done that much sound editing, I admit, but I'm guessing it follows the same principles as picture editing. I synched up a lot of dailies working on the *Genji* production. Make sure the sound goes with the images. Get rid of what's unnecessary. Make it flow. Bring up certain sounds here. Mute them there. I know I can do it.

The two fellows who wave me in don't look like artistic types. And for good reason. They produce newsreels. They're more hardheaded businessmen. They tell me they're running a very lean operation, and they're looking for a cameraman and a soundman. They want one of the two, either the cameraman or the soundman, to double as their editor. This sounds like a great opportunity, and I tell them I'm their guy. They say they have some tests for me to take and they put me through my paces.

I show them I know how to run a tape recorder and handle a boom mike. I know how to check the levels, so the sound quality is good. I know how to use a Steenbeck editing table and I synch up some film and sound to prove it to them.

Next, they pull out a machine I haven't seen before. It turns out it's to test my hearing. I listen to a series of pings and beeps and murmurs, and I let them know when I hear them. Obviously, to be a sound guy, it's important to hear well. If I ever have the misfortune to run into Poochie again, maybe I'll thank him for the great hearing he knocked into me. Maybe.

When they're done, they tell me to wait outside, and they'll be out in a minute. I think I did well. My hearing's sharp. I'm feeling pretty good about my chances. When the door opens, one of the interviewers comes out shaking his head. "Sorry, buddy," is his send-off. I start to say something in my defense, but he looks so set, I see nothing is going to change his mind. I just shrug and trudge on out of there.

I walk slowly out into the street and think about having to share the disappointment with Ariane. We're running low on cash. If we don't work soon, I don't know how we're going to survive. The initial excitement of returning to New York is draining away and things are getting pretty desperate. Ariane talked to a bookstore owner who said he would call her, but she hasn't heard anything.

I pass an Irish bar and a big cheer goes up inside. Guys are listening to the Yankees on the radio. The Yanks must be winning. I do something I don't normally do and veer inside. Sure enough, the place is crowded, guys are heated up, there's lots of hubbub. I find a spot at the end of the bar and order a beer. It's dark and loud, but I might as well be alone. I need to collect my thoughts, and this is as good a place as any. I've got to find work. The beer comes and the glass is cold, and it washes a little of my disappointment away.

Some big guy jostles me as he squeezes his way up to the bar. I try to give him some room and go back to nursing my beer. His beer arrives and foam's dripping down the side of the glass. Only then does he turn and face me, and I see it's the guy who gave me the bad news after my interview.

He smiles and says, "All right, buddy. Keep it down. We want you to work for us. Your hearing is off the charts. What are you? Part-canine?"

"My hearing's pretty good."

"No joke. Here's my card. Come by tomorrow morning and I'll explain."

"What's the job pay?"

"$22.50 a week."

"Nice."

"Plus tips."

I'm thinking to myself, Ariane and I can live on $22.50 a week.

"Tips?"

"You'll see."

"If you say so."

"All right, partner, down the hatch."

The big guy polishes off his beer and slides on out of there. I casually look around. No one's paid any attention to our short conversation. Gehrig's at the plate. More important matters are taking precedence. I inspect the business card I'm holding. Douglas Fitzpatrick, sergeant of the New York Police Department's Tenth Precinct.

I tell Ariane about the cloak-and-dagger encounter I had and the next morning I present myself at the Tenth Precinct. Fitzpatrick explains to me that they want me to help fight crime in New York City, which he informs me is rampant. He tells me there are more than a few of us $22.50 men working the city taxi routes. He says J. Edgar Hoover came up with the idea himself, and that the FBI's bankrolling it.

My Hudson is a luxury I can no longer afford. I unload it for a couple C-notes and start cabbing it.

CHAPTER 5

GOURMET FARE

The couple in the back of my cab are talking freely. They've no idea there's such a thing as a $22.50 man.

"I can't wait to get home to our bed," the man says wearily. "I feel like I've been sleeping in a life raft for the past week."

"Another minute on that ship and I'd have mutinied," his wife answers.

"Oh, I would hate to see you keelhauled, darling," the man murmurs, chuckling. "Can you believe the cheek of that customs man? Practically accused me of smuggling."

"That was so funny," the woman admits, laughing.

"Funny? He accused me of having a trunk full of sausages. What was that? Some kind of joke?" She keeps on laughing. "What's so funny?"

"I didn't tell you, but I put a few *saucissons secs* in your trunk at the last minute."

"You're kidding?"

"My bag was full like an egg. I would have asked, but you're a terrible liar."

"Thank you."

"You're welcome."

"Any other stowaways I should know about?"

"Don't be cross. You'll be the happiest one of all to have those sausages. I know how much you like them. Truth be told, you're also the proud owner of a couple bottles of Chablis. And a half-dozen ripe cheeses."

"I thought my trunk seemed heavy."

"And a few tins of foie gras."

"No wonder they were suspicious. Stinky cheese."

"Probably. But pawing through a steamer trunk's harder than it looks. A little French cuisine isn't going to kill anyone."

"You crazy, clever girl."

"Driver," the woman says sharply, "why are we turning here? We said West 72nd."

"I'm sorry, lady. I work for the NYPD, and I couldn't help hearing what you said."

"What the…?"

"I'm going to pull over for a minute, so we can talk."

Once I park the taxi, I pull out my badge so these passengers can get a good look.

"So, here's the deal," I say, laying it out for them. "Either I run you in for smuggling or you open your bags, hand over the contraband, and promise never to evade New York customs laws again. Promise, and I'll let you off with a warning this time."

"Outrageous!"

"It's up to you."

"The thought of all that rich food makes me feel seasick anyway," says the man. "All right, darling, you packed my trunk. Be a good girl and unpack it for the officer, so we can trundle on home."

"Do you really have to take it all? They're presents," the woman pleads.

"You seem like nice enough people. I'm sure this was an honest mistake."

"Definitely!"

"The health laws are what's important. Unpasteurized cheese is a big no-no. I'm sorry but I'm going to have to confiscate all the cheese. And the sausage."

"Oh."

"You can keep the wine and the foie gras."

"We are most obliged, officer," says the husband, who clearly thinks they're holding on to the truly fine fare.

"I don't enjoy this either," I say. "I turn it over to the guys at headquarters and they destroy it. It's a shame, but public health comes first."

The woman doesn't say anything to this. But she crooks an eyebrow and gives her husband a look that seems to call into question my truthfulness. When I stop at headquarters later, I bring the contraband delicacies to the office of one Sergeant Fitzpatrick. I explain why I'm there and he waves me in to see his second-in-command, a guy named O'Beckett.

"How are tricks, Laughaway?"

"Fine. I have some contraband to turn in," I say.

"Give it here," says O'Beckett.

I pull out a stack of French cheeses—Roquefort, brie, camembert, Morbier—and a bunch of hard sausages and lay them out on his desk.

"Where'd you find these?"

"Some world travelers brought them back from Europe," I explain.

"Damn criminals."

"I figure the health department will want them."

"They don't got time for this penny-ante crap. We'll dispose of it ourselves. Take one. Take your pick," says O'Beckett.

I hesitate. I've started a new life. I'm trying to go straight.

"Well, don't take all day. I said take one," O'Beckett growls. "Share and share alike."

"Sure, thanks," I say, giving in. I pick up a camembert and slip it in my jacket pocket.

"Don't got anything else, do you?"

"No."

"Okay, Laughaway. Keep up the good work. Serves 'em right. Lousy scofflaws."

When I get home, I present Ariane with a fresh loaf of bread that I bought on the way home and one perfectly ripe, freshly imported camembert.

"Yum. Jean-Yves, what's the occasion?"

"I met a couple fresh off the boat from Le Havre. I did them a favor."

"That was nice."

"I went out of my way for them."

"Isn't that what cabbies do? Go out of their way for people?"

"I let them off with a warning from the health department. First time I've gotten cheese for a tip."

"This camembert is ripe," says Ariane, prodding it with her finger. "Let's try it."

"Definitely."

"I want to visit my parents in Paris someday. Now that I know they're there."

"I would too, sweetheart."

I pull a bottle of white wine out of our icebox and open it with a pop.

"The wife was the mastermind. She smuggled a bunch of French food through customs… in her husband's luggage. He didn't have a clue."

"You're kidding."

"No. She thought he was too honest to lie convincingly. And it almost worked."

"Funny."

"She thought she'd gotten away with it after his luggage cleared customs. When they were safely ensconced in my cab and I'd pulled away from the port, she started laughing and let him in on her secret."

"That must have been some surprise," Ariane says.

"I tried to turn it all in to headquarters, but they strongly suggested I take something home. When I hesitated, the cop, O'Beckett, gave me a very dirty look."

"Hmm."

"Complications. But all is well. It'll be okay."

"I suppose we just have to enjoy it, before it turns into some big old health hazard," says Ariane, spreading the gooey, stinky French cheese on a hunk of bread and taking a bite.

CHAPTER 6

FLEA MARKET

New York is an expensive place, but there are ways to make do or at least a bit better. You can find life's necessities on the cheap at various flea markets. I have the world on a shoestring…

Ariane and I decide to look for some things we need one Saturday morning, and we make an adventure of it. Apartments in New York are generally tiny, which makes for a lot of not horrific things hitting the market all the time. No one has room for two. If people buy something new, they invariably get rid of something else to make room for it. That goes for books, too. There's only so much room.

We find a lively flea market at Broadway and Broome and naturally we gravitate toward the people selling used books. Ariane has an eye out for Chinese and Japanese books, and I have an eye out for old books, classics, rare books, first editions. I'm not averse to picking up something just because it strikes me as fun.

So, what do I find in the jumble of unwanted works? *The Home Bartender's Guide and Song Book*, published in 1931, when Prohibition was still in force. On the first page it reads:

"Published in sacred memory of those good old days when bartending was an exact science, and you could forget your troubles on any corner." I think it might come in handy and part with eight bits to add it to our library.

CHAPTER 7

LISTENING IN

Our luck takes another turn for the better. Ariane lands a job working in an Asian bookstore. She convinced them to hire her by suggesting they could get a direct line on some fine, rare Asian books via her connection to her grandmother's book shop in Los Angeles, the Dragon and the Lotus.

During the day I bomb around town, fighting traffic as if I'm forever charging out of the gates at the start of the Kentucky Derby. Every time the light turns green, all the cabs surge forward, the flanks of our cars practically touching. Whenever I break out ahead, I feel like calling back at the other cabbies: "Here's mud in your eye." And I keep my ears open.

At night we enjoy some tranquility, listening to music and reading. Sometimes I write, and so does Ariane. I'm writing a tale based on my former life in the dark, a story that culminates in our story.

I wish I'd met her earlier, but I had wandering to do before I walked into her L.A. bookshop with orders to buy a dozen copies of *The Tale of Genji*. Was it fate? Fate is what's already happened that you can't do a damn thing about. There's no such thing as what you might have done instead. There is no instead. We can entertain the notion that we have alternatives, of course, that our lives could have taken different paths. But could they have? You and I and everyone else you'll ever know trace a single one. This isn't a profound idea. It's self-evident.

The obvious question is whether fate applies forward in time and not just in retrospect. But how can we know? And is it imposed from outside or is it self-imposed? We make our bed; we lie in it. Or is our bed made for us? In fact, we can lie in it or sleep standing up. Or stay up all night.

You get born, you take a deep breath, and from that point on you've got a past, and it's only going to get murkier. Who are you going to blame? Everyone who's lived a day? Every one of us? I think I know less about Ariane's past than she knows about mine. Her life before in Shanghai. When I start to wonder too much, I ask myself what's the point and try to just jump off that mental merry-go-round.

Our apartment is a sweatbox. Ariane gets us a couple tall glasses of ice water. I hold mine to my forehead and to the side of my neck. They're both refreshing, the water and the cold glass. She tries to shock me by touching her glass to my back, but the evening's so hot her little prank is welcome.

When we decide to call it a night, it's still so muggy,

we have to give each other room in bed to keep from melting. Our shadows don't fear the heat, though. They don't ask for a little breathing room, and neither do our souls. I kick off the top sheet down to our feet. A tiny, lazy current of air pushes through the open window next to our bed. A mere puff every so often. We'll take it. The sweltering weather has come between us. I'm going to make up for lost time when the weather breaks. Ariane knows it's only a temporary, meteorological rift.

CHAPTER 8

A DENTED COCKTAIL SHAKER

One evening Ariane comes home a little later than usual. She pulls a box out of her satchel.

"We got our first shipment of books from my grandmother today. This was inside, addressed to me."

"What is it?"

"I don't know. I didn't want to open it in front of my boss," says Ariane. "Just in case…"

"Well, go on," I say. "Maybe it's a wedding present."

"Maybe."

Ariane gets a knife from the kitchen and begins carefully slicing the tape binding the box. Whoever put together the package used a lot of tape. Inside she finds a sealed letter and a beautifully wrapped present. She briefly turns the letter for me to see. It's written in Japanese. I wait as she reads it.

"It's from my grandmother. She's sent us $100 as a little wedding present."

"She's all right. Are you going to open that other present?"

"Of course. It's from my uncle."

"Oh, boy. What now?"

Ariane carefully undoes the wrapping paper and inside she finds another letter and some oblong object wrapped in tissue paper. She shrugs and opens the next letter.

"Well, how do you like that! My uncle sends his greetings and apologizes for getting our hopes up. Apparently, this isn't for us. He just wants us to hold on to it for him until he can retrieve it."

"Such a pal. Go ahead, Ariane, open it up. We might as well know what he's parking with us."

Ariane reluctantly tears away the tissue paper and lying there before her is a tarnished silver cocktail shaker.

"He didn't say we couldn't use it, did he?"

"No, he didn't, but the top seems to be stuck," says Ariane.

"Aha."

"Go ahead, Jean-Yves," says Ariane. "You can get the top off."

"Maybe it just needs a little elbow grease," I say, grabbing it firmly and twisting. Then I yank and strain. I pry. The top might as well be a barnacle.

It's a nice old piece. An antique. We'll polish it and add some luster to our apartment. But first I'd like to uncork it and press it into service. Here's where my study of chemistry comes in.

"I have an idea," I say. "Hot things expand. Cold things contract. Let's heat the bottom part of the shaker in boiling water and cool the top with ice. The base should expand. The top should contract. Then maybe we can get them apart."

Ariane grabs an ice cube tray out of the icebox, while I light the gas under a saucepan half-full of water. She dumps the ice cubes in a towel and holds them around the top of the shaker. When the water comes to a boil, our chemistry experiment is underway. After heating (and simultaneously cooling) the two parts of the shaker for about five minutes, I pull it out of the hot water, wrapping the bottom half with a towel to protect my hands. I begin rapping the side of the top against the kitchen counter, doing my best to dislodge it.

I hit the top pretty hard about five times and suddenly it flies off and clatters across the kitchen floor! We burst out laughing. But the shaker is full of paper and starts smoking as if it's about to catch on fire. I snatch the top off the kitchen floor and set it back on the shaker to snuff it out. Ariane and I give each other looks of genuine surprise.

"Better let it cool off. All that paper needed to combust was oxygen."

"I wonder what it is."

"If it's burned up, I guess we'll never know."

When the shaker is cool to the touch, I carefully remove the top again. I don't have to knock it against the counter this time. We look at the charred paper inside. Carefully I pull a paper bundle out and lay it on the kitchen counter. The paper is brown with age and black from having been burnt. I go to unwrap it and it crumbles.

Inside is some sort of scroll. It's about an inch in diameter and about six inches tall, red and gold. On both ends, the scroll is attached to a sooty cylinder. When we carefully wipe one off, it appears to be jade. It's carved with Chinese characters and depicts a dragon rising from a pool of lotus flowers.

We let it cool some more without trying to unroll it. Ariane studies the writing on the jade and tells me that it's not Chinese but Japanese. Deciphering the writing that's visible on the outside, she says it appears to have been written by someone who lived hundreds of years ago. The Japanese is archaic.

"'The Mystery of the Jade Scroll in the Bent Cocktail Shaker,'" I say.

"Or the mystery of how to drink from a fire."

"I wonder what your uncle's doing with it."

"I do, too," Ariane admits. "I'll see if I can read it. This is exciting! Now, how to unroll it without ruining it?"

"It's a tightly wound little secret. I hope your uncle won't mind... too much."

"Meantime," she asks, "how about a Manhattan?"

"It would be a shame not to try out this lovely old cocktail shaker!"

I pull a Maraschino cherry out of a jar I take from the icebox. Out come two cherries joined by their stems. I hold one of the cherries out to Ariane as if it were a wishbone.

"Want to wish on a cherry, *chérie*?"

"I do."

"Have you made a wish?"

"I have. And you?"

"I have."

We each gently tug until... Ariane comes away with both stems. She looks at me and smiles.

"Well...?"

"Well, what?"

"What did you wish?"

"I'm not supposed to say, Jean-Yves."

"Does it have to do with the scroll?"

"I'll let you know what I wished for, when it comes true."

"You want to hear what our *Bartender's Guide* said about Manhattans—and Manhattan—during Prohibition? 'Here's to you, Manhattan... may your towers ever pierce the sky, and may your cellars never quite run dry!'"

"That's funny. Cheers, sweetheart."

CHAPTER 9

THE CREEK THAT SANG

Over the next few days, we ply the little red-and-gold scroll with steam and then gently put pressure on it to get it to unfurl. Going slowly like this produces results and Ariane manages to unroll it far enough to reveal what she tells me is a poem.

"Maybe we should leave it be," I say. "We might ruin it."

"Not just yet, Jean-Yves. This is so interesting! It will be a marvelous translation for me to work on."

When I come home from work that evening, Ariane is excited to read me her first attempt at a translation.

"A woman wrote this," Ariane says. "How she learned to read and write is a mystery. Women in ancient Japan weren't often allowed to. This first poem is simple and beautiful and sad. I have your full attention?"

"*Oui*."

Ariane begins to read:

"'Why does the young gentleman
in the brown robes not come back?
He brought me a flower.
He fed me two pieces of rice cake.
And he smelled like a cool stream.
Why does he not come see me again?
I have only a stub of candle left.
I should blow it out,
save it for a moonless night.
I'm tired.
Maybe tonight the young gentleman will come.
That other time was late like tonight,
but there wasn't a full moon.
Maybe he prefers shadows,
like the creek I used to play in
that sang under the trees.'

"Do you like it, Jean-Yves?"
"It makes one wonder."
"It wasn't easy to read at first. But I think I made it out."
"It's amazing it's still legible. What a find."
"I know. I hope I can learn more about her."
"Her voice is quiet."
"It's been quiet for eons," says Ariane.
"I wonder how many poems there are."
"We'll see."
"Exciting."
"And here's this," she says, holding up a sheet of paper. "I made a fresh copy of the Japanese."

CHAPTER 10

MY THOUGHTS ARE A SNOWSTORM

New York is busy but it has an inner logic. Like some infinitely intricate gyroscope with a million moving parts. It's easy to be anonymous and alone here. We have a routine and it's a welcome refuge. That's how everyone tries to cope with all the activity. Ignore as much as possible and keep your own life as simple as you can. This is a peaceful, creative period for Ariane and me.

When I next get home (after listening in on my fares' remarkably laconic, inconsequential patter), she tells me she's been working on a new translation and wants to share it with me.

"These poems seem to be connected," she says. "Did I tell you that?"

"No, I don't think so."

"I began translating another. Can I read you what

I've been working on?" Ariane is holding a piece of paper and looking at me expectantly.

"Wait just a second, darling. Let me get out of my work clothes. I want to give you my full attention."

"Of course."

I rush around, taking things off, putting things away, finishing homecoming rituals.

"Okay, I'm ready now."

"They're not numbered, but my sense is this probably follows the first one I read to you."

"You have my full attention."

Ariane reads in her quiet, resonant voice:

"'I keep my poems in a lacquer box
under the old, stained cushion in the corner.
It's too cold for writing.
My thoughts are a snowstorm,
my fingers are brittle twigs.
I can hardly feel my paintbrush.
That fat oaf rapped on my door tonight.
He wore a thick, quilted robe.
His breath smelled of rice wine.
He recited a little love poem
and seemed pleased with himself.
When snow is blowing in the window,
I told him, a blanket is more beautiful than poetry.
He looked surprised.
Why the surprise?
He is simpleminded like a yak.
He called me his beautiful poem.

I wish he would bring me a comforter.
A mat and a blanket would keep me
from shivering like a wounded animal.
It's abhorrent, this dirt floor.
The night is dark blue, overripe,
like a smashed October plum.'"

When she finishes, she looks up expectantly to see if I liked her translation. I did. I do.

CHAPTER 11

THE CRASH OF 1935

Fifty short blocks uptown, the old gal—Pandora Racker—is impatient for the main bout to begin. Her husband, Jacob Racker, emperor of the fur trade, doesn't yet know that he's sharing the fight card with her. But he should. He ran amok yesterday evening and needs to pay.

After a tiresome dinner party the previous night, just as she's happily dozing off, there comes a heart-stopping wallop of a crash overhead! As if someone's inadvertently dropped an anvil. Then she hears her husband's footsteps coming down the stairs.

Judiciously, fearfully, he waits a few minutes before trying to join her in the marital chamber, stinking to high Heaven. That scullion's tougher than she looks. She rebuffed him. Him with his sly ideas. Sly as a rhino.

When he's undressing, the old gal puts him on the spot by asking him how he bruised his hip. He splutters out some nonsense, says he slipped and fell at the tannery. When he drops into bed, he practically crowds her off onto the floor. Now she really can't sleep.

Infuriated by his devil-may-care snoring, the old gal lies awake. Seething. The whole house heard him sprawling. And, yet, day after tomorrow, he'll have put his whole little setback behind him. Everything will be back to normal. That's what he thinks! It's intolerable. Impossible.

In the morning, Pandora Racker is still thinking bitterly about the cause of her unrest. Her husband and the new maid. Lotta. Pandora sees now, painfully, that the Irish maid is much too pretty to have around her husband. Tall, fit, hardworking. Well-intentioned, even. But too comely.

("A Lotta this... Lotta that..." Who gives a child an adjective for a name? She must have been the butt of a lot of jokes as a kid.)

Pandora realizes she made another mistake: lodging the help right over the master bedroom. What a crash! But the little room off the attic is already taken by the other maid. Do they need to have every extra room in the house filled with pretty, young things? You'd think they were living in a harem. She knows she asked for more help around the townhouse, but really!

This very morning, Pandora is going to lay down the law for Lotta, in no uncertain terms. No anvil juggling after midnight. Then she's going to start throwing haymakers in Round One with her poor excuse for a husband.

CHAPTER 12

KITCHEN WAR

When Lotta comes downstairs, Pandora Racker takes her aside. When Pandora tells the maid that she was awakened by quite a bump in the night, Lotta blushes, saying she tripped in the dark, that she knocked over her dresser. She apologizes a lot, covering up for her boss. Acting as if it's just an afterthought, Lotta asks whether it might be possible to lock her room? That she was scared at night. Pandora thinks this is a good solution and gets her a skeleton key. Lotta's relieved. No more uninvited guests for the pretty Irish maid.

When Jacob Racker descends for breakfast, the old gal decides to have it out with him. She's trembling, furious. Livid.

"I've had enough! Mauling the help. Right over my head!"

"I don't know what you're talking about."

"You don't? My eye. The morals of an alley cat. That's

your idea of fun, humiliating me."

"What's set you off like this, I don't understand."

"You do so. I want a divorce."

"Pandora."

"Divorce!"

He tries to calm her down, but she'll have none of it. Finally, against his better judgment, he gets tired of objecting. A fatal error.

"Maybe you're right."

"Oh, I am, am I?"

"Or maybe a little vacation. You could…"

Before he can utter another word, she picks up one of the crystal wine glasses from the dinner party the night before, which is on the kitchen counter waiting to be washed, and hurls it on the kitchen floor.

"No, no, no," he stutters. She immediately snatches up another glass and smashes it, too. She's just warming up. "Please stop." She lets fly another. "Stop breaking our crystal." And another. "Please stop breaking things."

"You wish!" She dashes the saltshaker on the floor. Next, she takes a light bulb that's sitting on the kitchen counter and throws it at him. For a split second, as it sails over his head, he looks like a cartoon character who's just had a bright idea. It dashes against a faded still life, a painting of domestic tranquility. Bits of glass spray down the wall and onto the floor, filling the kitchen with their own special musicality.

"Honey, I'm very tired," he says quietly. "One of my biggest customers is threatening to pull our contract. I don't want a divorce. You know it tears me to pieces when you talk like this."

Without deigning to reply, the old gal storms out of the kitchen. The maids, who can't help but overhear the couple's latest skirmish, are hovering in the doorway. The two of them make way as Pandora rushes out. She's won the battle and may well be on her way to winning the war.

"Sorry," he says to the two maids, looking sheepish, barely able to face them. "It's nothing. A misunderstanding. A terrible, unfortunate misunderstanding."

"Yes, sir," says Lotta.

"Of course, it is," says the other maid, Dora.

"The missus must have gotten up on the wrong side of the bed," says Lotta.

"That's right," says Dora. "Must have been the wrong bed."

"Yes, something like that," Racker agrees. "I trust you can take care of this mess without cutting yourselves. Am I right? Good girls. Well, I leave you to it. Easy does it."

With a half-hearted wave, he tries to tiptoe out of the kitchen, taking the swinging door on the wall opposite from the door through which his wife vanished. His departure is punctuated with the almost painful sound of glass cracking underfoot. The kitchen is littered with crystal. There's glass everywhere.

When he's gone, the two maids look at one another. They don't say a word. They know all about this kind of misunderstanding. The new maid, Lotta, raises her eyebrows, looking for a sign of recognition, but Dora, the one who's been there longer, just gives her a fish face, not letting on to anything. Deadpan.

"I'll clean up," Dora says finally. "You take care of the

bedrooms."

"Are you sure?"

"Yes."

Lotta knocks on the door of the master bedroom and the lady of the house appears, stone-faced.

"I'll change the dirty linen, if now's convenient?" Lotta asks.

"I wish you could," her mistress replies. "Now's as good a time as any. If you're going to air my linen, please do it in private."

Later that afternoon, the doorbell rings. Dora opens the door to Mrs. Racker's nephew, Otis, who's holding a large cardboard box, special delivery. Dora has met Otis before and lets him in, wondering if he wants to talk to his aunt or uncle. He says neither, no time, but he wouldn't mind a quick snack.

It's lonely working for the Rackers. Dora is happy to talk a little with a young man, someone more her age. She cautions him to watch out, there might still be some broken glass around. He sets the package on the kitchen counter and helps himself to some sandwich fixings and a glass of milk from the refrigerator. Dora continues carefully sweeping around the walls and under the cabinets to try to make sure she gets the last of the glass her missus broke that morning.

"You all get hit by an earthquake?"

"Not exactly," Dora replies. "A storm. Something set your aunt off."

"Good ol' Uncle Rack," Otis says.

"I suppose."

"Did she nail him?"

"No. Only his ego," says Dora. "He turned bright red."

"For good reason, I bet," says Otis.

"He doesn't make it easy for us to work here." Otis looks at Dora, expectant, waiting to hear more. "You know," she adds.

"The tannery's tough, too. I like it better here. I've been getting horrible headaches since I started there."

"A good night's sleep, that's what I recommend."

"I'm half-asleep now. I just got off a ten-hour shift tanning. But Uncle Rack called. Needed an express delivery," he says, lowering his voice, taking a gulp of milk. "Wanted me to bring Pandora a present. A peace offering from his shop."

"Oh, he got her a fur!"

"Mink."

"Hmm. Lucky," says Dora.

"She doesn't seem that lucky," he says.

"No, I guess not," Dora admits. "What do you do at the tannery?"

"You know all the leather coats you see people wearing? I'm the genius behind all that," says Otis.

He gives Dora a can-you-believe-it look, raising an eyebrow, taking a big bite out of his sandwich. Dora finishes sweeping up some last bits of glass and dumps them in the trash.

"I don't know if I already told you. I'm Otis. Auntie's nephew."

"I'm Dora."

"Nice to meet you, Dora," Otis says. "We've met before, right?"

"Maybe."

"I've got a few irons in the fire at the moment," he says. "I'm not going be a tanner all my life."

"Is that where that smell comes from? I'm sorry, I don't mean to…"

"We're like chemists."

"Well, put your dish in the sink when you finish. I'm sorry but I've got more chores to do. I better be off."

"Okay, Dora. Make sure my uncle gets the package. Tell him I would have said 'hello,' but he's keeping me too busy. I'm going home to bed."

"The missus will like this a lot, I bet," she says, picking up the box and departing.

When Otis is alone, he leans against a counter and scans the kitchen. He isn't in any condition to see his aunt and uncle. His head feels like it's on fire. He lifts one of his feet and looks at the sole of his shoe. There's a chunk of glass stuck in it. Carefully he extracts it and sets it on the counter next to him.

He gets some ice from the fridge, runs it over his brow, and holds it to his temples. Water trickles down his cheeks and down the front of his coat. As he's thinking things over, finishing his sandwich, he hears voices and footsteps. He holds the ice to his throat then pops it in his mouth. Despite his vacant expression, he looks as if his tongue's in his cheek, but it's just the ice cube melting. He wishes he could slip it straight into his scalded brainpan.

CHAPTER 13

FASHIONING A GOBLET OF HEMLOCK

One day in late summer I come home to find Ariane, pensive, pen in hand.

"What are you thinking about, Ariane?"

"Justifiable homicide."

"Ahh."

"My ancient poet is sharing thoughts of revenge," Ariane says.

"Really?"

"Let's see. I've done a preliminary translation of several poems today. I've been busy." She straightens her papers, then begins to read:

"I don't remember being happy,
maybe I was long ago.
Before.

Before that and long before that,
and before then and then. Maybe then."

In another poem, she wonders who will ever read her writing. Will anyone ever find it and read it? And will they care about the thoughts of a poor, lonely, literary woman?

"I'm living in layers of loneliness.
Even my aches are aching deep in my muscles,
all through my tired heart.
I'm like a bell that winces whenever it's rung."

To spite a bad man who visits her, she dips her hand in her ink and pats him on the back of his kimono, leaving a handprint for his wife to see. The woman comes one night to find her.

"She tried to hit me in the head
with my own lacquer box.
My poems spilled instead.
Some landed in a puddle on the floor
and the ink ran. Some life.
Thank God I woke up in time
and blocked her arm and my cache of poems,
the weight of words.
I hope she doesn't tell anyone about them.
She probably couldn't read them anyway.
She stormed out after trying to hurt me.
She did hurt me, more than she knows,
ruining my poems.

The $22.50 Man

Maybe I can recopy them.
I don't know how I'm going to get more paper."

"A man with black hair and a scar
came and got rough with me.
I bit him and he pulled my hair hard
to get me to stop.
I might as well be half-bald.
I'm so angry.
I keep crying.
I wish I could drown him in mud,
or worse, an ocean of his own tears.
Maybe I'll fashion him a goblet of hemlock
and let him poison himself
as he likes, at his leisure."

CHAPTER 14

THE PARADOX OF THE INTIMATE

Next day the boss tells me he's got a new taxi for me. This kind of news I don't argue with. He takes me into the parking lot and shows me what he's talking about. It's a shiny yellow cab, basically immaculate. I'm surprised at my luck but try not to let on. It's still a cab. It still means taking directions from all of humankind.

"Anything special I need to know?"

"Don't bang it up, Laughaway."

That night I drive it home. It's roomy, smells clean, and practically floats over the potholed streets of New York City. The shocks on that other jalopy I'd been driving were completely shot. Felt like a bucking bronco. This feels like I'm in the Thanksgiving Day parade. I almost feel like rolling down the window and giving people that wave, the slow, regular one you're supposed to give people lining the streets when you're in a parade, like a metronome or a windshield wiper. Or the queen. But I'm supposed to be keeping a low profile, not acting like some lunatic, so I stick to business.

A woman, who looks vaguely familiar, flags me down and I pull over. I feel kind of gallant in my new car, so I open the back door for her, but she surprises me by climbing in the front seat instead. She's wearing a pink cotton dress and a light coat. She rearranges herself and God help me, her dress gets hitched up a little for a second. Blue. Satin. Fringed with white lace. Light blue.

She looks down in a hurry at the glimpse she's given me and makes a show of tugging on her dress. Then she turns her eyes back on me, speaking a universal language, the one she uses I guess when she wants to be well understood. I take a deep breath. What is this great good fortune of mine?

"Where to, young lady?" I ask her.

"I leave that to you." Well, well. She's French.

"Okay," I reply.

I ease the car away from the curb and we float into the slipstream. My passenger shifts herself slightly again and slides just a little closer to me. It's such a huge front seat. Her pale blue satin, unveiled for a second, reminds me of a break in the clouds. A line of poetry. A tiny electric heavenly sky.

"Boy, this heat is terrible," she says, her voice thick, breathing fast, trying to control herself, sound natural. "Who needs a coat? What a ridiculous idea!"

"It is warm."

"It's of no use," she says. "Off it comes."

"I'll put on the fan."

My new taxi is equipped with a little electrical fan that's mounted on the dashboard. When I turn it on it begins to swivel left and right, like a palsied fellow trying to decide whether it's safe to cross the street. It moves the air around some.

I guide the yellow chariot through the city's night-thick streets until we come to a deserted side lane. My passenger has slowly and surely moved next to me during our ride. Her shoulder is touching mine and I can feel the light pressure of her thigh. I park and she looks at me and we begin in earnest to find out how comfortable this new cab really is. And the nature of the sky's fabric, and the unlayering layers of night.

The sky quiets and gathers and the windows of the cab cloud over. From out of our darkening trance, she reaches back with her right hand, and it bangs the window behind her. She pulls it away and smears the fogged glass, drawing me a sweep of shooting stars, shooting stars I can't wipe off.

"Do you like my new auto, Ariane, darling?"

"I do, Jean-Yves. But it's you. You're what I like, as you well know."

Later, whenever the car steams up, I see Ariane's hand reaching back and

The $22.50 Man

bumping the window, marking it with the once-and-for-all gesture of a Zen painter, the infinite echo of a wordless haiku.

CHAPTER 15

A WHALE WASHES ASHORE

Ariane looks unmistakably serious when she comes home. She tells me she's gotten another letter from her grandmother. L.A.'s Little Tokio apparently had a complete disruption of its water supply, which meant everyone was suddenly without water. A disaster anywhere, but decidedly in L.A. in summer.

The city engineers were called in. At first, they thought a whale had swum into the culvert supplying drinking water to the greater Los Angeles area.

What they found could have been Moby Dick, it was so great and so white. Or a colossal albino gecko. They eventually determined it wasn't a whale or a bloated gecko. It was a well-known gangster, a mob boss. And he seemed to have been shot before going swimming. In the back.

Big Department had turned up. A known lieutenant of the Green Gang. An international drug trafficker.

The $22.50 Man

Now, according to Ariane's grandmother, Little Tokio is swarming with cops and questions, and everyone is struck dumb.

I've had premonitions before. Ever since I fell off my Aunt Simone's balcony. But tonight I have a dream unlike any that I've ever had before or since. If it's a vision of things to come, I'm sorry.

I find myself tumbling in a fight with night and shouting and war, wrestling darkness and threats of violence, dizzying clouds of confusion and menace. It's as if I'm completely engulfed in someone else's psyche, someone else's madness. A terrible cracking noise shatters over me. I'm roiled in an avalanche of frenzy and pandemonium.

With a jolt I come to. You bet I do. Can't take dying lying down, even in our dreams. Ariane is there next to me! Plain-as-day reality feels like a benediction, a huge, deep breath of fresh air. Oh!

I'm not anxious to fall asleep, only to find myself back in the same berserk phantasm. I lie awake, instead, listening to Ariane breathing and the stray night sounds of New York City, hoping it's only a nightmare this time, not a premonition. But I don't really buy it, considering how visceral it was. It was more of a coming attraction than a dream. Someone else's madness.

CHAPTER 16

52-CARD PICKUP

The other cabbies are regular guys, driving for a living, not expecting much. Most are card sharks. When they're not driving, they're taking each other's money playing poker. I play a little at first but I'm no good. It's unprofitable. I go back to reading over lunch. But I do witness one truly memorable hand between two diehards. One's a big, irascible guy named Artie. The other's a small, wiry guy named Dizzy. I'm not sure what his real name is. Dizzy, it turns out, is afraid of heights. Since "claustrophobia" and "acrophobia" are too fancy, they start calling him Dizzy and the name sticks.

I know about this firsthand because one afternoon I'm heading into the Empire State Building to pick up a fare and I run into Dizzy. He's pacing around the lobby, agitated, and, boy, is he glad to see me. He rushes over and begs me to deliver a package for him. He'd rather die than climb in that elevator. He was stuck there, until

I came along. I'm his savior. Poor guy.

So, here's how the game of poker goes down. Dizzy and Artie are playing a hand over lunch, and they both have killer cards and they're betting heavily, raising each other repeatedly. Finally, they run out of cash to bet, and they turn over their cards. Dizzy has three aces, but the big guy Artie turns over a flush. Five diamonds.

In one motion Dizzy grabs the cards and flings them in the air. They ricochet off the ceiling and scatter all over the place. Reminds me of standing on Fifth Avenue in a ticker tape parade. Artie just smiles and laughs a little. The boss catches this act and yells at Dizzy: "Hey, clean that up. What've I said about 52-Card Pickup? No 52-Card Pickup!"

The little guy shouts back: "Artie can pick 'em up. They're his damn cards," and out he storms.

Artie breaks into a huge grin. "Seeing him throw those cards like that was great. That takes the cupcake. That was better than winning his dough."

CHAPTER 17

GETTING DIZZY

Some days over lunch I work on my book, jotting ideas down in a small notebook. This eventually arouses the curiosity of that big galoot Artie.

"Watcha doin', takin' notes about us?" he wants to know.

"Nothing like that," I say. "I'm working on a book in my spare time."

"A book, huh? What's it about? Me?"

"No, it has nothing to do with you, Artie. You can read it if I finish it, if you want."

"So, it's a mystery."

"You could say that."

"Always knew there was something mysterious about this guy."

"Ah, leave him alone. You couldn't write your own name if we spelled it for you," says another of the cabbies.

"Oh, yeah?" Artie says, starting to get pissed.

"He can't be a complete illiterate," says Dizzy. "He can read the signs."

Artie clenches his fist. "Whatta ya make of dis, Dizzy?"

"Wrong way?"

You don't want to get on Artie's lousy side. He seems to get worked up in a hurry. Like a lot of cabbies, he turned to driving by default, after washing out of quite a few other honorable professions—the army, jukebox repair, lamppost painting. Sooner or later his temper soured the deal.

Word had it he walked off his job as a painter after a run-in with "the quality." An upstanding citizen, decked out in a top hat and tails, made the mistake of passing within spitting distance of our colleague, who at the time was slapping paint on a lamppost from the top of a ladder. The swell took umbrage when a big fat drop of paint splashed onto his suit coat. For a second, he probably thought it was a pigeon. After he realized what was what, he started grousing and our esteemed colleague explained the situation to him by dumping the whole bucket on him. That's when the big lug walked away from his true calling. He just left the ladder where it stood and retired from the arts. Which earned him his sobriquet.

"Okay, I admit it," I say. "I was just trying to sound interesting, Artie."

"Huh."

"I was making a list. The stuff I need to grab on the way home. Takin' care of business."

"Takin' care of funny business."

"I forget otherwise. Who can keep track? Let's see…

Coffee, soap… and, now that I think about it, cat food."

"Famous last bullshit. I been doin' somethin' interestin' lately myself," says Artie. "Bought myself a new Harley. It's so beautiful I could hump it."

"Who's stopping ya?" Dizzy asks.

"Not you, tiny, that's for sure."

When the meter's running in my cab, I'm engrossed driving and listening. It's shocking the stuff you hear. The people who come down the gangway and climb in my cab are so tired after crossing the Atlantic, they practically talk in their sleep.

CHAPTER 18

SALT GRINDER

Back uptown, Pandora has cooled down a little. Fall is here. The maid gave the peace offering to her boss—a pure white mink stole—and then Racker presented it to his wife with great fanfare. Mink seems to have done the trick. For now, once again they're imperfectly reconciled.

Today's latest battle is more trivial. It concerns salt. Salt and high blood pressure. And breakfast. This time it's she who's giving in to his demands, but not without a few parting shots.

"You want salt. Have salt. Have all you want. You want to kill yourself? Be my guest."

"Why spoil my appetite? I can't eat steak without salt."

"I can't watch. I'm going upstairs to see how I look in the mirror. I'm going to go play with my new pet."

"You'll look regal, my queen."

"It is nice of you. Thank you. It'll keep me warm.

This cold snap is worse than some of my moods," she says, laughing, as if to forgive him for now, partially blaming herself for overreacting, throwing him a bone. She's always throwing something.

After his wife departs, Racker grabs the salt mill. He tries to turn the grinder, but it doesn't budge. What now? Frowning, he gives it a shake and tries again. This time it turns, loudly, and he gets what's coming to him. He makes sure he doesn't miss a spot. He relishes the sight: salt glistening on a juicy New York steak. His mouth is watering. He cuts himself a piece. Medium rare. Perfect. Finally, after all that guff, breakfast. Steak and eggs.

Then a lilting voice sounds in his ear: "Excuse me!"

"Huh?"

He stops in midair and turns. Lotta, that cute Irish scullery maid, is practically serenading him; at the same time, she's practically flying or diving onto him, but no, she's not, she's doing a kind of dance, now she's even doing a pirouette. He tries to shovel a bite of steak in his mouth while watching her bizarre, impromptu performance, but she's too fast for him. She swoops up to him like some avenging angel and deftly snatches the fork out of his hand.

"Hey! What do you think you're doing, you impertinent…!"

She lowers her voice and whispers with great urgency: "Quick! Now's our chance! No one's around. Give me a kiss, quick…"

Jacob Racker is surprised, to say the least, but for a second, he is truly and absolutely distracted from the call of the belly. Lotta leans down toward her boss, now moving ever so slowly, practically mesmerizing the poor, stricken fellow. And as she bends down, unbelievably, to give him a kiss, he looks up, wide-eyed, grateful, and eager as a baby bird about to taste the long-awaited morsel, and she closes her hand around the salt grinder and lays it quietly across his breakfast plate, along with the fork she whipped out of his hand with the yet untasted piece of New York steak. Then, as she gets within inches of his frankly shocked face, she braces herself and gives him a peck on the cheek.

Moving into a much quicker gear, she continues to pirouette, whisking the plate out from in front of him, doing the "Shuffle Off to Buffalo," practically tap-dancing her way out the swinging door and into the kitchen. She calls back over her shoulder to say she'll be right back, but she seems to miscalculate. With infinite lack of grace, she trips, and his beautiful breakfast flips out of her grasp and scatters all over the floor. She watches intently as the plate bounces, bounces, and then shatters. The fried eggs splatter first. The steak slides into second. The salt grinder rolls all the way to center field. And there in the middle of the once inviting breakfast is a fork still skewering that first nice big piece of juicy steak.

Racker is left sitting by himself, looking in wonder at the blank expanse of white linen where his breakfast used to be and should be still. The clatter of his meal tumbling is the last straw. When he pushes aside the swinging door into the kitchen, Lotta is down on her knees, smearing egg yolk around with a kitchen towel.

"What the hell?"

"I'm sorry! What an idiot I am! I thought your

breakfast could use more spice. A little kiss… I went to get some pepper… I can't believe I tripped!"

"Good God!"

"Would you like some cereal?"

"Are you out of your mind?"

"It's good for you. It's healthier than steak and eggs anyway."

"You're bleeding…"

"Oh! You're right. I must have cut myself on the plate…"

"Well, take care of your hand. Clean that food up later."

"I'm such a klutz," Lotta says, looking at her bleeding hand and fingers.

She gets up and goes to the kitchen sink to run warm water over them. It smarts. She tries rubbing her fingers together gently, trying to extricate the glass that's still pricking her fingertips.

"It's not serious. Don't worry. I'll be all right."

Her boss sidles up behind her and puts his arm around her waist, giving her a squeeze. "Well, Lotta, thank you for spicing up my day."

"I'm sorry."

"Never mind. I'll get breakfast downtown. I'm meeting the mayor this morning."

"I'm sorry!"

"Don't apologize. Wish me luck. And take care of that cut. What a madhouse!"

When he's gone, Lotta turns away from the sink, letting the water run, and looks long and hard at the food lying in the middle of the kitchen floor, and especially at the salt grinder. No one comes to see what all the fuss is about. Not the old gal. Not the other maid. Everyone's occupied. Lotta turns back to the sink and keeps picking glass out of her skin. Her fingertips are covered with tiny bleeding cuts.

She presses a towel to her fingers, trying to get them to stop bleeding, and surveys the mess on the floor. The house is strangely quiet, as if people are holding their breath. She gets back down on her hands and knees to erase the debacle. Then she retrieves the salt grinder. She opens it and dumps the contents into the garbage. Several large flecks of porcelain fall out, along with salt and ground glass. She knocks it several times to make sure it's good and empty. She notices she's left a smear of her own blood on it and grabs a towel to wipe it off. Right then the kitchen door opens and the old gal steps in, followed by the other maid, Dora, wanting to know what all the racket is about.

"I had an accident with the breakfast. I spilled it," Lotta confesses.

"What are you doing with that?"

"I was going to refill it. It's empty."

"That's a good one. Not a grain of salt left after he's done with it. Did he get enough to eat?"

"No, not really." As Lotta says this, she looks carefully at the old gal and the other maid to see how they take the news.

"No? After all that?"

"I know. I'm sorry. He didn't get too angry. He said he'd eat downtown."

"What happened to your hand?"

"I cut it picking up the plate I broke. I'm sorry about the plate!"

"Gad."

It's hard to tell whether the old gal's looking at her with such hard eyes because she's wasted good food or for some other reason. The other maid looks on impassively. Lotta excuses herself to take care of her bleeding fingers. She locks the bathroom door and looks at herself in the mirror. She looks terrible. She patches herself up with some Band-Aids. As she's coming out of the bathroom, the other maid, Dora, suddenly appears around the corner and gives her a weird look, squeezing out a dry greeting before climbing the stairs.

Lotta has had enough. She goes to her room to get her things. She locked it earlier and now she can't find her key. Tough! She won't spend another minute in this place. She'll call for her things later. She tiptoes back down the staircase, past the study where the old gal is looking out the window, down the front hallway to the door. Quietly as possible, she picks up a few loose coins lying on a desk by the door. She'll need them for the subway. Then she slips out, shutting the door as quietly as she can.

It's cold outside. But it has a brisk, bracing feel. She hurries down the stairs and into the street. People are streaming by. If they notice that she's woefully underdressed for such a cold day, they must figure she's somebody's maid dashing to the corner store, picking up a missing ingredient for lunch. She adopts the air of a woman who knows her business.

Thankfully, it's warmer down in the bowels of the

subway system. She remembers the train that used to take her to Queens. And there it comes roaring up. She shivers, shakes herself, and steps across the gap inside. The car is crowded and steamy, filled with damp passengers. She grabs a strap, wraps her other arm around herself, and dances a little from foot to foot, making the cold just bearable. Did the old gal see her wiping blood off the salt grinder? She knows he tried to maul me the other night. Probably thinks it was me, taking revenge. But it weren't me. I'm never going back for my things. I can do without. Evan'll help me. I pray he's home. He wasn't a bad guy, just a reckless, stupid gambler. What if he doesn't live there anymore? I pray he still lives there. I'll take his attention off cards.

CHAPTER 19

THE MAYOR

Jacob Racker is a substantial fellow, but even so he looks diminished waiting to see the mayor. The chairs in the reception area are too small for a man of his girth. He's having trouble getting comfortable. He glances at the morning paper and his watch.

A woman finally opens the door to the inner sanctum. "The mayor will see you now, Mr. Racker."

He extricates himself from his chair, grabs his briefcase, and follows her inside where the mayor smiles familiarly and waves him in.

"Jacob."
"Mr. Mayor."
"Sit down, sit down."
"Finally, one my size."
"Can I get you something?"
"Whatever you're having."

The mayor gets up and pours them a couple of

drinks, handing one to Racker.

"You know, Mr. Mayor, it's not too late in the season to get in a round of golf at my club."

"Good idea!"

"By the way, I didn't forget that the last time we saw you, you expressed admiration for a little something my wife was wearing. It's nothing, really, but I thought your better half might enjoy something along these lines, now that fall is here."

Racker pulls a box out of his briefcase and pushes it across the desk in the mayor's direction.

"Oh, what have we here? May I look?"

"Absolutely."

The mayor opens the box and finds a beautiful white mink wrap inside. It is one of those long, thin numbers that a woman can throw around her neck. He strokes the fur for a few moments and remains silent.

"If you don't think it's her style," Racker says hurriedly, "tell her she can come pick out whatever she likes."

"Now, that's right white of you, Jacob. Not that she won't love this little thing, but you know what winter's like here in New York. She might prefer a little more protection. I'll talk to her. Thank you. You're a real New Yorker."

"Greatest city on Earth."

"What do you say we go have that sit-down with the chief? He's expecting us."

The mayor slides the gift into one of the drawers in his desk and gets up.

"I've got to warn you," the mayor continues, "the chief's got some new idea that he's all wound up about, and I'm not sure I can unwind him. But no need to be a wet blanket. Let's go team up on him and we'll see what we can do."

"But I thought you were the one who makes the decisions around here."

"Normally, yes, but this affects the chief's men. He's pretty adamant that he's got to give his okay, too."

"I understand. Of course, he does."

They climb into a cab outside, and the mayor and Jacob Racker, tanner and furrier, continue their conversation.

CHAPTER 20

TALK OF SHOES

Earning my extra $22.50 a week depends on a few things—sharp hearing, an ability to read between the lines, and just plain, dumb luck.

Today is one of my luckier days, seeing that I get hailed by a couple of New York's power brokers—Jacob Racker and the mayor. They're deep in conversation about something that matters to them both—shoe leather.

"Why is the chief changing his mind like this?" Racker asks, sounding agitated.

"He says he's thinking about his budget…"

"Well, Mayor, doesn't he want quality?"

"Some Chinaman pitched him another idea. The chief thinks it deserves consideration."

"What's the guy got cooked up?"

"We'll discuss it when we get there. Something about rubber."

"Rubber? I'm offering quality leather. Real leather. Cowhide of the American variety. You know that."

"I'm sorry, Jacob, to interrupt. I seem to have forgotten my wallet. Would you mind getting this?"

We're outside police headquarters. The mayor-with-no-wallet climbs out of the cab while Racker digs into his pocket and hands me a crumpled five-spot. He doesn't wait for the change, which is all right by me.

They head for the front door as if they own the place.

CHAPTER 21

FLAT-FOOTED

When the mayor and Racker arrive at the office of the chief of police, there's no waiting this time. They're immediately ushered in to see the head of the force.

"Mayor."

"Chief."

"Jacob."

"How are you, Chief? Keeping our jails full?" the mayor asks.

"I always try to keep a cell or two empty, for special occasions."

"No need to make any special arrangements on my behalf," says Racker, inspiring the mayor and the chief to smile. But only a little.

"How's the missus, Chief?" the mayor asks.

"What're ya bringin' her up for, Christ Almighty?"

"Well, you know, with winter coming, Jacob here can be a real godsend. He just offered to let my little lady come by and pick out any fur in his warehouse. Maybe he'd do the same for you, Chief. That might warm your gal up."

"Oh, I tell you, it would," Racker enthuses. "You should have her give me a call. Our tailoring is tops. We'll make her something that really decks her out."

"Gee, thanks, Jacob. I'll do that," says the police chief. "But I'll save that for the right moment, you know, when I need a boost."

"Don't wait too long," the furrier says. "Now's the time. It won't have the same bang next summer."

"I won't. Thanks. That's a nice thing you're doin' there. Well, here's the thing. I know we've used your services for several years now, but money's tight in the department. The Depression's still killin' us. I got a call a while ago; I told the mayor a little about it. A Chinese guy asked to make a proposal of his own. Said he represented some muckety-muck with big holdings in Asia. Shanghai or Rangoon or some damn place. Rubber plantations. He came by and showed me the niftiest rubber soles ya ever saw."

"You're throwing me over for some guy from Rangoon?"

"We've tried 'em out, you know, put 'em through their paces," says the chief.

"You're letting some flatfoot make the decision? Jeez, after all I've done?"

"Who ya callin' a flatfoot?"

"I didn't mean anything."

"If my men have flat feet, who do ya think's to blame? You're the shoemaker."

"They're the highest quality you'll find, Chief."

"Well, in wet weather, these gumshoes, that's what he calls 'em, they hold up better than leather. And they're cheaper."

"Oh, Lord. You're killin' me."

"Maybe you can trim a little off your price, Jacob," says the mayor. "It'll make you more competitive."

"How much do I have to come down would you say?"

"Or make a donation to the mayor's reelection campaign. And the Police Guild. And the retirement fund," says the mayor. "I'm not suggesting anything extravagant. Just to foster some goodwill, you know. Very worthy causes."

"Of course, I will. That was always my firmest intention," says Racker. "I'll send you both some marvelous winter gloves we're creating this year. They'll keep you snug."

When Jacob Racker departs police headquarters, he doesn't feel like jumping in a cab. He isn't in any hurry to get back to the office. Instead, he turns on his heel and begins walking slowly and thoughtfully, his head swimming with Oxfords and rubber soles and gumshoes and flat feet. Things didn't go as smoothly as he'd hoped, but he can still salvage the situation. For one thing, he'll just have to lose big the next time he and the mayor play golf. Bigger than usual.

CHAPTER 22

LOTTA TROUBLE

That same day, over another game of poker, Artie lets drop that he went by Dizzy's place one time and there were padlocks on everything. The bedrooms. The cupboards. The dressers. At first Dizzy starts to deny it.

"My place ain't like that."

"No?"

"That was my mom's place. Before she threw me out."

"Ah."

"The craziest thing's happened," says Dizzy. "I've acquired a houseguest."

"Saving on your rent?"

"Maybe someday. My ex-girlfriend showed up at my door yesterday."

"Lucky you."

"I hear a knock, answer the door, and there she is, standin' there shiverin'. No suitcase. No dough. No coat!

Wearing a flimsy dress in this weather! And that's everything she has in the world. That and goose bumps."

"Jesus. What's her story?"

"I'm still trying to figure it out. Something to do with a fat cat from the Garment District. Lucky I wasn't on my shift."

"Hmm."

"We broke up a while ago. Lotta drama. Never thought I'd see her again. Then there she is, big as the noonday sun. No one else to turn to but me. Lucky I was home."

"Is she a looker?"

"Yeah."

"You still sweet on her?"

"Oh, hell, yeah, but I'm as broke as she is. I try to bring her down easy as I can that I'm not flush. What's she say to that? She says: 'Why don't you talk to those fellows you know in Brooklyn, get money from them?' Get money from them! Makes it sound simple. I owe them money already! She's got no idea what she's talkin' about. Those guys are already squeezin' me dry."

"What's your gal's name?"

"Lotta."

"Lotta what?"

"Probably a lotta trouble," another cabbie says.

"Lotsa luck," says Artie, starting to deal another hand of poker. "Sounds like you're gonna need it."

"You know," Dizzy says, "I've always had a lotta luck. Proof. She came back."

CHAPTER 23

BE FOREWARNED

Later that week, the Big Overcoat gets a handwritten note in the mail. Short and to the point:
"Dear Mr. Racker, this is no prank. Someone is trying to poison you. I hope I'm not too late telling you. And whatever you do, lay off the salt! (Signed) A concerned citizen."

The Big Overcoat quickly puts the letter in his pocket. Poison! This isn't the type of communication to leave lying around. I'll tell the old girl it was from the office. Need me to come in, look over the books. Concerned citizen, my eye! It's a girl's handwriting. Maybe it's somebody's idea of a joke. It says it's serious. Must be that new maid. Talking about avoiding salt. My old maid now. Old maid. Hardly. So cute. Gave me that kiss. I come home, can't wait to see her, and she's gone. And she hasn't come back. Left no phone number, no address. Left all her things. She was in a hurry. I'll make some inquiries. Find

THE $22.50 MAN

her. Find out what got into her.

How can she know someone's trying to poison me? Did she taste it herself? She'd be dead, instead of me. She must like me, warning me. If it's really from her. Granted, the old gal was crazy. Smashing the crystal we got when we were married. She's threatened to poison me before. If I ever tried to leave her. I thought she was kidding. A grim little joke. Not that funny. I might have to stay in the other apartment for a while. Or go on a business trip. I could stay in Wellsboro. Tioga County, Pennsylvania. The tannery. Talk about a choice of poisons. I'd rather eat the old gal's pot roast. There's that one hotel that's not too bad. It's got that bar and the nice barmaid. I wonder if she's still there…

As he pulls on his raccoon coat and balances a homburg on his big head, he calls to his wife up the stairs, "Sweetheart? I'm off. Urgent business. Have a nice day!"

"Go to hell!"

Now what have I done? He makes sure he has his wallet, and after thinking otherwise, he pulls out some money and puts it on the table by the door. When he leaves, he shuts the door quietly, firmly. He pulls his hat down, fingers the letter in his pocket, and takes a deep breath. He hails a brand-new yellow cab.

CHAPTER 24

TRAVELING IN STYLE

My big yellow taxi attracts a lot of welcome attention these days. Left and right people are flagging me down as if they know me. So, it comes as no surprise, when I'm trolling for business in Midtown, that a big fellow gives me the energetic wave of a long-lost friend. It turns out he almost is.

When he climbs in back, I recognize him as the mayor's companion. The beefy cobbler. Life is strange.

"Where to, mister?"

"23rd and 2nd Ave."

"Okay."

"Say, on second thought, if I pay you for a round trip, could I hire you for a longer ride? You wouldn't have to wait around when we get there."

"Where do you want to go?"

"Tioga County. You know it?"

"Not really."

"It's in the Alleghenies, in Pennsylvania. Wellsboro, to be exact."

"Pennsylvania! How far are we talking about here?"

"About two hundred and fifty miles…"

"And you'll pay me double the meter when I deposit you?"

"That's my offer."

"Okay, sure. It's a deal. Would you like to listen to the radio?"

"No, thank you."

"If you don't mind my asking, what're you heading to Pennsylvania for?"

"Business."

"What line are you in?"

"Furs. And leather."

"What kind?"

"Mainly raccoon. I've got trappers all over and I own a tannery in Wellsboro. Big operation. The tailoring we do in the Garment District."

"You don't say."

"People have been making leather goods there for a long time. I have a big operation."

"How many raccoons does it take to make a big overcoat?"

"Half a dozen. It depends on their size."

"They must scramble off the rack this time of year."

"It's seasonal. Far as I'm concerned, the weather can never be too bad."

"Lucky you."

"I'll make you another offer. Go easy on the price today and I'll make you a deal on a coat, knock the price way down. You got a girlfriend?"

"I'm married."

"That's tough."

"Not really."

"Give it time."

"How long have you been married?" I ask the big guy in the back seat.

"Too long. That's the impression I'm getting, anyway."

"My wife's a poet," I say. "And a sometime actress."

"I know a few theater people."

"Really?"

"One of my relatives is in theater promotion. He's always looking for new talent."

"My wife is beautiful and brilliant. She's part-Japanese and part-French."

"An exotic beauty!"

"I think so."

"That would take a special kind of role. A lot of the stuff playing on Broadway these days isn't that exotic."

"No?"

"Not from what I can tell. You know what my bread and butter is? Shoe soles. My company holds the contract to supply the soles for all the police shoes that traipse the five boroughs. The police walk around, doing their rounds, on my fine cowhide."

"Nice."

"It used to be a very steady business. The cop on the beat does a lot of legwork. No matter how sturdy we make 'em, they wear 'em out. That's the beauty of it. They always need more and more and more new shoes."

"I won't look at those flatfeet the same again."

"Looks like I'm in for some tough negotiations this year. Competition."

"Well, good luck."

"Maybe you'd like to try the fur business. We can always use dependable workers."

"I like driving, but you never know… maybe."

"If you want to put on the radio, some classical music, that would be fine. No news. Something soothing."

"No problem."

"You wouldn't have anything to eat, would you? I've had the craziest mornings lately. Yesterday, I was just about to tuck into my steak and eggs and our maid dumped the whole setup on the floor. The day before that my wife threw a fit. Today I got called away on urgent business. The breakfast gods are conspiring against me."

"What did you say your name was?"

"Jacob Racker."

"Mr. Racker, it's your lucky day. It just so happens I've come into possession of a sizable cache of *haute cuisine*. Do you like French food?"

"Love it."

"Okay, hold on. We'll get ourselves a few little items to make the trip easier on the system and then we'll feast on the move. How's that sound?"

"Splendid."

I pull over, pop the trunk, and begin rummaging through the gourmet food I confiscated from some luckless travelers earlier that morning. I return laden with dry sausage, pâté de foie gras, various kinds of cheese, two bottles of slightly chilly rosé, and a bottle of cognac. My passenger shows all the signs of a fellow who's unexpectedly found himself safe inside the pearly gates, even with the meter running.

    Next, I pull up to a bakery I know and return with three loaves of bread, cups, and napkins. I pass him back my knife. And a corkscrew. When I hear the first cork pop, I ease back into traffic and I point us toward Westboro or Wellsboro or some hell-or-another, Pennsylvania. Jacob Racker and I are becoming pals. By the time we get to the tannery, he's been asleep in the back seat for an hour.

CHAPTER 25

A SHAMBLES

Racker's factory in Tioga County is a shambles. He invites me inside to take a gander, seeing that we've broken bread together on the trip. He thinks maybe I'd like to move up in the world, leave taxi driving behind for the leather trade. He admits it's a union shop.

Only then do I realize what it means for a place to be "a shambles." A shambles literally is a slaughterhouse. I can't get out of there quick enough. The place is something straight out of the *Inferno*, except the animals are the damned and the workers are the devils. For a minute, they look as if they're all carrying pitchforks. The smell is revolting, an acrid amalgam of dead animals and fresh-cut trees. Racker assures me one gets used to the work. When I'm about to leave, he gives me his card and asks me not to tell anyone where I've dropped him.

As I'm leaving, I hear a noise coming from a corner stacked with boxes. Out of the boxes stumbles a skinny guy, who veers toward me, snickering and talking to himself. I guess you don't have to be completely sane to work here. He says something about catching forty winks. He must have been sleeping back there behind the boxes.

A guy yells at him: "Hey, Otis. Your uncle's looking for you."

He doesn't say anything, just smiles as if he's leering at something and swaggers away, as if he just remembered where he's going.

I think about my conversation with Racker as I drive back to Manhattan. It's hard to meet theater people driving a hack. I got his card. Maybe he can help Ariane land an audition playing somebody's maid. Or the girlfriend of Dr. Fu Manchu. Maybe we could mount a play of *The Tale of Genji*. Racker gave me two $100 bills for the round trip and the fine food.

CHAPTER 26

NEW YORK STEAK

During a break in his shift, Otis the Brick goes looking for his uncle, who is about to tuck into a quiet supper in his office. After a moment's hesitation, Otis invites himself to sit down at his uncle's repast and gets a baleful look from the Big Overcoat.

"Uncle Rack, that's a lot of beef…"

"This ain't the steak that's gonna kill me, Otis."

"Auntie says you need to go light on the salt!"

"A few little grains of salt can't hurt. I've got a cast iron stomach."

"She's not worried about your gut. It's you blood pressure, Unkie. And your heart."

Racker gives his wife's nephew, Otis, a long look. "Do you like working at the tannery, Otis?"

"Ha."

"I told you it wouldn't be all fun and games. You look like hell."

"The union thinks you should give me some of your big, mouthwatering steak. That it would be good for both of us."

"I know they do. But where to divide? How much do I share? Where do I cut? Here? Here?"

Otis draws a line in the air over his uncle's slab of beef. "Here!"

"It's dispiriting, to say the least, how people keep coming between me and my steaks. First your aunt. Then Lotta. Now you."

"You wouldn't miss it if you gave me a little slice. I'm awful hungry and that looks so good."

"As my special assistant, you're not in the union, Otis. But just to show I understand the plight of the working man, I'll give you some. Pass me a plate over here."

Racker proceeds to trim a small strip off his steak and puts it on his nephew's plate. "There. Now eat up and get back at it. You've got things to do, right, if you want to earn your paycheck? In the future, save your nickels and buy your own damn steak!"

CHAPTER 27

SOME MUG

When I get home from my journey to Wellsboro, Pennsylvania, it's plenty dark. I'm tired. The wine and cognac have worn off and I feel kind of crummy. I collect the remains of our repast from the back seat. I'm thinking about getting home to Ariane and telling her about my trip with the tanner when I hear a kind of rushing sound behind me. Someone's in a big hurry to meet me. I turn around fast and there's a big mug standing there with a knife in his hand. He's just kind of showing it to me, jiggling it a little in case I'm the unobservant type.

"Gimme yer fuckin' money" is all he says.

New York has its perils and here's one. It's too late to do anything but fork over my dough.

"Okay, okay. Gimme a second." My heart is pounding. I go to pull out my wallet and the guy gets jumpy on me.

"Easy does it, fella."

"I'm just getting out my money."

"Step on it."

I pull out my wallet and hand it to him. I don't want him to think I'm studying him for the police lineup later. I'm hoping this transaction will be over with quick. He's not getting away with a fortune or anything.

He gives me a bloodshot look and turns back the way he came, walking quickly in the direction opposite that of the one-way street. A guy across the street seems to be his lookout and he slips away, too. I lock the cab and duck inside. Ariane is understandably mortified. It's too late to call the police. Those guys are long gone.

Happily, I'd slipped Racker's $200 in my sock before heading back to Manhattan, just to be on the safe side. When I retrieve it and unfold it on the table in front of Ariane, she starts to cry and gives me a real squeeze.

CHAPTER 28

CAUGHT IN FLAGRANTE DELICTO

I tell my story at work and every guy has a tale of his own. A lot have been held up by passengers. They go to collect, and it turns out they're the ones who end up paying for the ride. That afternoon, my boss buttonholes me, says he's heard about the stickup and that maybe he has an idea how he can help catch the guy. I don't see how but I hear him out.

"What happened?"

"I was getting out of the cab and the guy came up behind me. It was dark. He had a knife."

"Did he say anything?"

"'Gimme yer fuckin' money.' Classic."

"Anything else?"

"I guess we exchanged a few words. Along the same lines."

"All right. You're all right, right?"

"Yeah."

"These guys move around. I doubt you'll see him again."

"Good to know."

"It'll be a different guy next time."

"Swell."

"Most drivers carry guns."

"So, basically, when I drop people off, I should be prepared to stick 'em up."

"I'll let you be the judge."

Later, when I return to the depot for a break, the boss waves me over. I follow him into his office, and he has me pull up one of his battered chairs. Then he brings out a gadget and turns it on.

"Listen to this. Do you recognize anything?" The machine is running and it plays a recording of me getting mugged.

"I didn't tell you. Your new cab is kind of an experiment. It's got a voice-activated recorder."

"What the...?"

"Car doesn't even have to be on. When someone says something, it starts recording. The door was still open when the guy robbed you, huh?"

"Yeah, it was open."

"Well, there's some pretty good evidence if the cops catch this guy. Also, that was quite a conversation you had with that guy you took to Wellsboro."

I was wondering why I got a new cab. Now I know.

"I won't play 'em the beginning of the recording."

"What do you mean?"

"The part with you taking your girl for a spin." The blood rushes to my head.

"Give me that recording. Anyone needs to hear me getting mugged, I'll have it."

"All right. It is kind of private," he says finally, with only a trace of a smile, and slowly hands it over.

"Thanks for not telling me I was being recorded."

"I meant to tell you. Now you know."

"When do I get a tour of my recording studio?"

"Later, when all the guys aren't around."

"Okay. It would be good if I knew how it works."

I shove the recording in my pocket and bang back out of there. I almost run into the big guy, Artie, who's standing outside the boss's office. He gives me the dead eye with just a hint of something alive. Was he listening? My cover as a $22.50 man might just have been blown.

When I go to sit down at my beat-up desk, Artie calls over to me good and loud.

"Hey, buddy, it's your lucky day. Your wallet turned up."

"Really?"

"Yeah, a Good Samaritan returned it. Bad news is you're broke."

I go over to collect my stuff. He hands me my wallet and my license, a few other slips of paper that must have been tossed by the robber. Artie takes his time before giving me one last card. He looks at one side, flips it over, scrutinizes the back, and only then holds it out for me to take.

"Mystery solved," is all he says. It's my police ID, the one they gave me when they hired me on.

I take a look, see what it is, and say: "That's ancient history. I washed out a long time ago. I just keep it in case I get pulled over for speeding."

He looks unconvinced. Then he says way too loud for my taste: "A $22.50 man, huh?"

The guy's trouble.

Later, when Artie's out on his shift and we're alone, Dizzy reassures me that Artie's not that bad if you never have anything to do with him. Then he tells me that he's also making an extra $22.50 a week. Now that's interesting. A couple weeks later I invite him and his gal over for dinner, so we can talk some more, out of earshot.

CHAPTER 29

LOTTA EXPLAINING

It's a Saturday night and Dizzy and Lotta ring the doorbell of our apartment at 7:00 o'clock sharp. They've gotten themselves spruced up and are in high spirits. Dizzy looks happier than I've ever seen him at work, and Lotta's really quite a beauty. She's wearing an odd maroon shift of some sort, smiling and laughing. Ariane and I make some spaghetti and we all tuck into it over a bottle of red wine. We exchange the usual pleasantries and questions. Ariane's story wows them.

"I emigrated from Shanghai, China, but I'm not Chinese. My father's Japanese and my mother's French. The Japanese military started attacking Shanghai. I had a chance to get away and I took it."

"Are your parents here in New York, too?" Lotta asks.

"No, my understanding is that they're in Paris," Ariane replies. "It seems I'm a citizen of the world."

"My family's all back in Ireland," says Lotta.

"Mine are in Brooklyn," says Dizzy. "My mother anyway."

"Mine are still in Montreal," I say, "as far as I know."

"Where'd you two meet?" Lotta asks. "Seeing that you're coming from different corners of the Earth and all."

"We met a thousand years ago in Japan," I say.

"Hooboy."

"I'm kidding. We met in Los Angeles. Ariane was working in a bookstore called the Dragon and the Lotus and I was working for a movie producer. We were shooting a film based on a thousand-year-old novel called *The Tale of Genji*."

"It was written by a woman, Murasaki Shikibu," says Ariane. "It might be the first novel ever written."

"I went to pick up some copies at a bookstore and there she was," I continue. "Pure luck."

"It's a beautiful book," Ariane says. "It was written when Japan was enjoying a peaceful period. People could think about things besides war and survival, like music, art, and poetry."

"You know why my boss wanted to make a movie out of it? Because it's sexy and it wasn't under copyright," I say.

"So, he was a high-minded type," Lotta says, laughing.

"Lotta and I were neighbors," says Dizzy. "That's how she bumped into me or I bumped into her."

"It's funny how people meet," Ariane says with a smile.

"Or meet again," says Lotta.

"There's a lotta luck involved," I say. "Obviously, what matters is whether we recognize it."

That's when we hear Lotta's story about why she left her job and found Dizzy again.

"My employer threw a big party, and everyone had gone home but the missus. I was in bed on the verge of falling asleep when I heard my door open, and someone comes in shushing me to keep quiet. It's my boss. I'm terrified. Straightaway he tries to climb into bed with me. He was so sloshed he missed it. When he hit the ground, the whole place shook. I turned on the light by the bed and there he be, without a stitch on, looking like a soft-boiled egg!"

"Or Humpty Dumpty," says Dizzy.

"What a nightmare," says Ariane.

"That's not the end of it. A couple days later, I go to put salt on my oatmeal after serving him his breakfast and I spill some on the table. I'm a superstitious gal, meself, so I go to toss the salt over my shoulder to ward off the devil, throwing it in his eye, and something stabbed me terrible. I looked down and my fingers were bleeding. It wasn't salt. It was glass! I ran to the dining room to stop Mr. Dumpty from killin' himself. I decided to distract him by giving him a kiss on the cheek to take his mind off food. He liked that," Lotta says.

"I'm sure he did."

Lotta tells how she whisked Racker's breakfast out from under his nose and then accidentally-on-purpose scattered it over the kitchen floor. She thought what he didn't know wouldn't hurt him. Or what he didn't eat wouldn't.

"At the same time, he was very annoyed to lose his steak. But I spared him some terrible indigestion, I tell you. He howled and called me impertinent. I couldn't tell him what was really happening. Whoever tried to murder him was there in the house. The old gal, his mistreated wife, or that other sad little scullion, Dora. I decided to get away from there. Next thing you know they'd have been accusing me. It was my fingerprints on the salt grinder. My blood. They even saw me trying to wipe it off, when I was cleaning up the mess." Lotta takes a breath. "Can you blame me?"

"Are you kidding? You had to do something," I say.

"That was pretty neat, how you did it," Dizzy agreed. "I wish you'd thought of something besides giving him a kiss, though. The bounder."

"If anything would get his attention, that would," says Ariane, trying to help.

"She couldn't have the guy sprinkling glass on his steak," Dizzy says. "It just ain't done, not even in Queens."

Lotta can't help looking at her fingertips, seeing how all the little cuts are healing. She lightly touches them with the pad of her thumb, one after another.

"You're a friend in need, Evan," she says, looking at Dizzy. That's the first time I've heard his given name.

"He was way out of line. How'd you get mixed up with this oversize overcoat, anyway?" Dizzy asks.

"I don't know. After you and I broke up, I bumped into him somehow. I was looking for work. He hired me as a maid," Lotta explains. "He told me I might meet all sorts of... What did he call them? Impresarios. Told me he had a relative who was a big shot in showbiz."

"Ariane's an actress," I say.

"You are?"

"Sometimes. I enjoy it."

"Sounds like your typical 'producer,'" Dizzy scoffs. "Those guys can only play that game so long."

"What's this guy do, living-wise?"

"He makes fur coats and shoes."

"A tailor, huh?"

"He owns a mink farm somewhere."

"How'd you say you met this guy?"

"He introduced himself to me."

"No doubt."

"His townhouse seemed like a safe place to get by for a while. After I'd been there a few days, he hinted he might give me a fur coat if I was nice to him. The only fur I ever saw was the back of his raccoon coat heading out the door."

"You should have worn one yourself out the door when you left," Dizzy says.

"Maybe I should have. He practically owed me one anyway for being such a cad. What choice did I have? I had to get out of there."

"You did the right thing," says Ariane.

"That's not too bad a business. Raccoon coats. Some of my fares wear them. You get two in the back seat, and it looks like you're driving a pair of grizzly bears to the circus. Yeah, and you don't have to go upstate to find raccoons, either," I say. "You can catch plenty right in the Garment District. Surprise them when the whole family is eating out of a dumpster."

"The guy's a weasel," says Evan. "Maybe he has a

weasel farm upstate."

"You took pity on him," Ariane says, trying to comfort Lotta.

"My God. He's so lucky," Lotta says. "He had no idea. I hate to think what that glass woulda done."

"I'd cut back on salt if I were him," I offer.

"No kidding."

"Especially if it's ground glass."

"Who do you think did it?" Ariane asks.

Lotta just shrugs her shoulders, looks at the floor, and shakes her head.

"He sounds like the gentleman I drove to Pennsylvania the other day," I say. "And to police headquarters. There's a coincidence for you."

"That's amazing."

"If it hadn't been for you, Lotta, I would have missed out on my biggest fare ever."

"You're welcome," she says, laughing.

Ariane and I suggest we move into the living room for a nightcap. It's a congenial evening. We get along. Dizzy tries to interest us in a little poker, but we assure him we'd be no competition, which probably makes it even more painful that we turn him down. He just laughs.

Dizzy changes the subject, asking me: "Heard anything crazy lately?" This must be a universal topic among $22.50 men.

"A lot of people are dead silent in the cab," I say. "They get in, tell me where they want to go, and then not another word. But every once in a while, people blab like I'm on planet Mars. But I'm not, and my hearing's almost too sharp."

"Mine, too. That's how I got the gig in the first place," says Dizzy. "Once I heard two guys talking about robbing me! I pulled my gun on them first and told them to get the hell out of my car. Couple of idiots."

"That's terrible!" Lotta says.

"It wasn't that big a deal."

"Really?" Ariane exclaims.

"You're not the only ones getting an earful, you two," says Lotta. "I heard quite a few things working as a maid. 'The quality' act as if you're not even there half the time. So, Ariane, what do you like to do when you're not selling books?"

"I'm doing some surveillance, myself," she replies.

"You're kidding."

"I'm translating some poetry from Japanese into English. It's as if I'm listening in on the poet's conversation with herself."

"What is she saying?" Dizzy wants to know.

"Well, the poems I'm deciphering at the moment are pretty dramatic. The poet seems to be a woman and she's contemplating murder."

"Ariane's translation is beautiful," I say. "In spite of the homicidal overtones."

"*Merci, chérie.*"

"I'd like to read it," Lotta says, "when you're done."

They want to know how she happened to take on the project and Ariane tells them about the scroll in the cocktail shaker. She doesn't tell them that she got it from her uncle.

"I've always wanted to find a treasure like that," says Lotta. "All I ever find are things with chips and cracks and stains. Kinda like me."

"Don't be silly. Look at how beautiful you are!" Ariane says.

"You're nice. Evan, I like your friends!"

"I'm thinking of turning it into a play," says Ariane. "The poems tell a story so far."

"I've never been to a play on Broadway," says Dizzy.

"Neither have I," says Ariane.

"I'm too busy dancing to the sound of the taxi meter." He trails off. "You know how it goes."

"I'll invite you. I'd love to have you come," says Ariane.

"I'm game," he says.

"What theater are you going to be performing in?" Lotta wants to know.

"Ah, that's a good question," Ariane says. "We'll have to see. Probably a little one. Off Broadway."

"Sure you don't want to play some cards?" Dizzy asks. "How about I deal a few hands and I'll walk you through them?"

CHAPTER 30

A PRINCE

Ariane spends the evening working on a new translation. She asks me if I'm ready for a surprise. How can I be? It wouldn't be a surprise if I were. She tells me that she subjected the paper scroll to another steam session and that she was able to unroll it a bit more. Its latest revelation is a shocker. She shows me the ancient text, open to its latest secrets. She points to the passage that she's translated. Then we sit down together, and she opens her notebook and begins to read aloud:

> "The young man knocked
> on the door to my hut tonight
> and smiled to find me alone.
> It was a moonless night again.
> He said he'd been thinking about me
> and that he couldn't not come here.
> I told him I was glad.

The clouds bowed down,
charcoal and brown,
not wanting to miss a word.
He said he wants to help me
get out of this life.
He said he'd like to lay down his cloak
so that I can cross the muddy path
from my seaside home
without my sandals touching the ground.
He said he was a prince. A prince!
I lit my last tiny candle
and asked him to say it again."

Ariane gives me her excited look, her mouth half-open. I'm sure my eyes are as wide as hers.

"The young man might be a prince," Ariane says. "Can you believe it?"

"I don't know, darling. Can you?"

"I've thought all along that this was a poetic journal. Some poor woman's thoughts… from centuries ago."

"It could be fiction. Or a forgery."

"Yes, maybe."

"But maybe not. Maybe it's her true story."

"That's my point!" Ariane exclaims. "That's what's so exciting! I couldn't believe it when I read this new fragment. I wonder who she was?"

"Maybe it's time to talk to an expert. Or a museum."

"What would my uncle say? I'd rather keep unraveling it myself. I love this project. I love having it all to myself."

"I understand, sweetheart. We need to preserve your

scroll while you tease out its secrets."

"I want to tease out your secrets," Ariane whispers.

"I don't have many secrets."

"I'd like to believe you. But how I can be sure? I think I need to take a closer look," she says.

And how can one know? If you have secrets or not, your answer will be the same: "I don't have any secrets." The person who has secrets and wants to keep them will deny it. And the person who doesn't have any secrets will deny it, too. If you take people at their word, no one has any secrets, and everyone is an open book or an open window. I wonder sometimes what secrets Ariane has from her life as a sometime actress in Shanghai, but as time goes by I have less and less desire to delve into her past. I'm of the school of thought that people have a right to their past. It's up to them to bring things up, if they want, when they want.

CHAPTER 31

THE POET'S DREAM

Ariane continues to translate the scroll, and her latest discovery is a centuries-old dream that the poet recounts. After dinner she informs me she has a new, longer poem to read to me. A dream. We sit down side-by-side on the couch, under an excellent reading lamp, and she begins:

> "Last night I dreamt
> my mother told me an old tale
> about a salt burner's daughter.
> The girl was poor as sand,
> ragged and sooty. Like me.
> One day a huge wave destroyed everything.
> The salt burner sent his daughter
> to search for dry kindling
> so they could boil seawater again
> and make salt for their livelihood.
> She walked away from the shore

and the land was unrecognizable.
She hiked into the hills
and came upon a narrow passageway
in a boulder cracked in two
from whence a thin stream of water ran.
She followed the trickle of water
to its source and found a pool
of fresh water overflowing.
She was overcome with the desire
to wash off the soot and the salt,
to drink all the water she wanted,
to give her clothes a good rinsing.
As she was bathing
a man came upon her
and told her he was a prince
and that these were his lands
and this was his pool.
She was terrified and asked him
to please leave her alone.
He said he wouldn't think of it.
He'd never had such an interesting
creature swim into his pool
and he wanted to study it
and then he wanted to catch it.
She refused his light talk

and swam to the far edge of the pool
where she snatched up her clothes
and tried to pull them on
without getting out of the pool
and having to reveal herself.
The man ran over and laughed
as she struggled with her wet clothes.
She gave up and tried to turn away.
As he reached out,
managing to touch her cheek,
she gradually turned to salt.
As she dissolved
and crumbled into the water,
the prince turned into a waterfall
and plunged in after her.
The gray cloudy waves of salt
streamed down the mountainside
only to be caught
in the drying channels of salt burners.
Her father stared into the evaporating water.
The steam reddened his face
as he boiled away the water,
distilling the precious salt.
There in the dry white crystal
he saw the clear outline of a hand,
the hand of a prince,
a man who thought he had the right
to take anything or anyone,
a man who had no more grasp
than a waterfall."

CHAPTER 32

1,000 YEARS AGO, IN JAPAN

It's evening and our apartment is crowded with friends, including Dizzy and Lotta, and even some customers from Ariane's bookstore. They've come to see the premiere of her play. We've drawn the curtains to block out the streetlights and muffle the sound of traffic.

Ariane comes out in front of everyone to give a brief introduction. She's wearing a light pink kimono and is looking quietly excited.

"Just a few words about tonight's entertainment," Ariane says quickly. "This is an experimental piece. It's a combination play, poem, and movie. The story is based on ancient poetry—from Japan—that I've been translating the last few months. Don't ask me who wrote it, because so far, I don't know. The film is footage left over from a movie we worked on in L.A., based on the classic

Japanese novel, *The Tale of Genji*."

There's a smattering of applause from the audience.

"It's a work in progress," Ariane continues. "For now, I'm calling it 'The Mystery of the Ancient Scroll in the Bent Cocktail Shaker.'"

People laugh at the ridiculous title. Someone chimes in "Cheers!" before being shushed.

"However, I may well call it 'The Salt Burner's Daughter.' I warn you, some of it is rather daring," Ariane says, widens her eyes, and purses her lips as if she's mildly shocked herself. Then she looks in my direction and gives me a nod. "I couldn't have done it without Jean-Yves's collaboration. Enjoy."

As Ariane withdraws, I turn off the lights in the apartment and ease past the end of a row of spectators, taking up my post behind a movie projector in the back of the living room. Friends shift in their chairs and wait quietly for this experimental show of ours to begin.

I turn on the projector to light the "stage," the far end of our little apartment. An INTERTITLE reads "1,000 years ago, in Japan." Ariane comes out wearing a ragged, dirty gray kimono, framed in the flickering light of the whirring movie projector. We've hung a white sheet at the back of the living room to serve as the movie screen.

She sits down at a low table, where she begins writing on a small scroll of paper. The ends of the scroll spill off either side of the table onto the floor. One half is filled with her writing. The other awaits inspiration. Her hair is disheveled. She uses a paintbrush that she dips in a hollow stone inkwell.

We HEAR a recording of her reading one of the

poems from the ancient scroll we found in the cocktail shaker, as if she's composing it in the moment. We hear her ruminate about the elegant young man who visited her one moonless night and brought her rice cakes. Accompanying her voice can be heard waves and seagulls (which we recorded in my cab on the waterfront).

A small candle sits on the table, lighting her at her work and tossing about some shadows. She gets up and walks the floor and looks out of a picture frame that represents a window. A crescent moon, cut out of white cardboard, is pasted on the dark paper in the frame. After lingering at the window, she returns to her table and continues thinking aloud about the young man.

She's interrupted by the SOUND of an older man's voice. She rises slowly, reluctantly, and disappears into our hallway. I turn the projector off. Our apartment is now quite dark. A truck barrels by outside and the driver lays on his horn. Our friends can't help but laugh a little at the anachronism, the intrusion of twentieth-century New York. After a few moments, we HEAR the sound of a different man's voice. I turn the projector light back on. Now I project a film that Ariane and I made of us together lolling around in bed. We spent an afternoon shooting us in slightly different positions, a few frames at a time. The resulting film is blurry and chaotic and luminous.

Ariane, my sometime actress, comes back onstage, passing back and forth, back and forth, before exiting again, and the film of us jitters and shimmers and jumps across the far wall of the apartment. It's impossible to see us clearly, which was the point. It's what we were hoping it would be. Evocative.

Finally, Ariane returns, looking as if she's sleepwalking. She pauses at her writing table to rinse the ink from her brush, swirling it in a small cup of water. The ink turns the water black. Any inspiration she had has long passed. She refashions the shape of the bristles with her fingers, laying the brush down next to the scroll. Then she blows out the candle and lies down on a thin mat in the corner. She recites the poem of poisoning her john with a drinking cup carved of hemlock. I turn off the projector. After a few moments, I turn on the lights in the apartment. Ariane has slipped offstage. Our friends give her performance a hearty round of applause.

"Intermission," I call. "Act II, the conclusion, will begin in about twenty minutes."

Everyone gets up, stretches, and heads to the kitchen for refreshments. The kitchen's only big enough for a few attendees at a time. Meanwhile, Ariane readies herself for her upcoming scenes. I fill glasses and we toast her work so far. I excuse myself and go to our bedroom, where I find Ariane lying on our bed with her eyes closed. She sits up when she hears the door open.

"You've been wonderful, darling," I tell her.

"Really?"

"Yes. Everyone's enthralled."

"Oh, good. I'm going to close my eyes and concentrate for a few minutes," she says. "Let me know when you're ready."

I give her a hug and return to the living room, where I change film reels. A film is a kind of scroll, too. I hadn't really made the connection until just now. I carefully feed the film leader into the projector, advance it a bit, and thread it into the take-up reel. When Ariane reappears in the door of our bedroom, I give her a nod to let her know it's cued up.

"Seats, everyone. Act II will begin shortly." When everyone's seated, I switch off the lights in the apartment, take my place behind the projector, and begin the second reel. This is a completely different film. Instead of the flickering light and the frame-by-frame nudity we used to light Act I, what appears now is more professional. It's the footage I kept from the production we did in L.A. of *The Tale of Genji*.

Ariane comes onstage and sits down to write at her low table. The film appears over and behind her. In the film, an entourage of Japanese servants and soldiers on horseback arrive silently as if from Heian Japan in 1000 AD. From the door of our apartment, an imperious voice announces the arrival of the prince. Ariane looks toward the door, alarmed, and jumps to her feet. After hesitating for a long moment, she moves toward the sound of the voice.

As she's about to exit, another actor, an elegantly dressed young man, steps inside to meet her. (I've left the projector running and have moved to our apartment door, where I can let in other performers.) She sinks down before him, hardly daring to look up. He takes off the tall black hat that he's wearing and sets it aside. Ariane looks up and smiles hopefully, timidly. It's the young man from the poems she's been translating. He reaches out both hands to her and lifts her to her feet. We see their lips move in conversation, but we cannot hear what they're saying at first.

Now a series of INTERTITLES convey their words:
"My name is Genji. I am a prince."
"Oh, oh."
"I am returning to Kyoto. Today."
The INTERTITLES end and the stage is bathed in the projector's warm white light. Now we hear the actors.
"What are you telling me?" Ariane whispers.
"I want to take you with me."
"You do?"
"Yes. My exile has been lifted. The emperor, my father, is recalling me to court."
"The emperor is your father?"
"Yes. Your exile is ending, too."
"But look at me."
"My attendants have everything you need."
"No. It's impossible."
"What? Why?"
"I can't return from here. Even your great arms can't reach all the way to these shores."
"Don't say that. The imperial city awaits you, your beauty, your poetry…"

We're hanging on their words when there's a violent thump on the apartment door, followed by what sounds like clumsy scratching, as if someone is trying to find the doorknob in the dark.

I open it cautiously this time. A wild-eyed man is standing there in a grimy bathrobe, carrying a cup in his hand. His black hair looks like sea grasses flattened in a storm. He has a long scar on one cheek.

He shoulders me aside and takes three steps into the light of the stage. Ariane sees who it is and begins shaking, backing away from him. He points at her and croaks, "You. Myrrh…!" He drops the wooden cup he's carrying, and it bounces toward her and the prince. We all stare. Someone in the audience gasps and cries out. Before anyone can say anything more, he pitches forward onto the stage with a crash and appears to expire.

Ariane shrieks and shrinks back down toward the ground, retreating like a crab to the farthest corner of the stage. The actor playing Genji gives the fellow a cool look. He turns toward the door, which I open, and shouts instructions. Two attendants enter quickly.

"I was forced to kill this intruder just now," Genji says. "Dispose of him."

The two attendants take the dead man by his arms and legs and carry him out.

"I know that man," says Genji. "He was a great nuisance. An enemy of mine."

"I'm horribly sorry," says Ariane.

"You don't understand. You have done me a service. You saved me the trouble."

"I must get away," Ariane states.

"Yes, of course. That's why I came."

"It's not your fault," says Ariane. "You've come too late. It's impossible."

"But it's not true," says the prince.

"I need to get away from the world," Ariane replies. "Have your most trustworthy servant take me to a monastery. In the mountains. Where I can meditate and write and disappear."

Genji makes as if to approach Ariane, who is crouching on the floor, barely raising her head to look at him. As he takes a step toward her, she turns her face away from him. He stops short. Then he turns away, too, and gives instructions to his entourage outside. A woman attendant enters our apartment with a kimono folded over her arm. She puts a hand on Ariane's shoulder. Genji exits. I slide back behind the projector to turn off the movie light.

We HEAR a recording of Genji reciting a passage from the poet's scroll:

> "'Even a dying flower resists.
> You want to rid yourself of me,
> but I won't make it easy.
> Pick up a faded bouquet gently,

> and try to toss it away.
> The petals will fall off
> on the floor
> at your feet.
> It's the same with you and me.
> You can only bid me farewell
> a few petals at a time.
> I love you. You love me not.
> Farewell, but only
> a few petals at a time.'"

I turn the projector back on and play the final film images accompanying Ariane's play. It shows footage of Genji's attendants and horses riding off into the distance. Ariane gets to her feet and the woman puts the kimono around her shoulders. Some of the film plays on their figures. Then the scene and the room go black. Our apartment is filled with applause. After a long ovation, I switch on one of our reading lamps, and the actors return for their kudos. First the attendants, the two men and the woman. Then the dead man, returned to the land of the living. Then Genji. And finally, Ariane, who gets sustained, enthusiastic applause. Lotta and Dizzy enjoy it. He wants to know what happens next. I tell him that's up to us to imagine, adding that maybe the untranslated part of the scroll will eventually tell us.

CHAPTER 33

AT LARGE

The expression "*prendre le large*" is the French equivalent of "heading off into the wild blue yonder," except one's traveling by water rather than air. When Poochie and Finnbar shoved off in the yacht they stole from Charles Granyer, the film producer I was working for, they were escaping L.A., sailing toward the horizon—vast, indeterminate, unknowable—as large as large can be.

They were headed where things are so vast it might be easy to become invisible. A wise move, given how outsized Poochie is. As far as I knew, they were still "at large." Anything to avoid its opposite, the straitened circumstances of jail.

One night I go to pick up some business on the waterfront and who do I see coming down the gangplank? A guy whose size is hard to miss. Poochie. He and his Irish friend, Finnbar, are lumbering down the ramp with duffel bags slung over their shoulders. Like a couple of old salts.

A number of us taxis are lined up and to my horror, they join the queue of passengers looking to grab a cab. I slump down in my seat, shove some sunglasses on, and pull my cap down a little. I try to make a quick estimate of whether I'm going to be the lucky one who gives them a ride.

You ever had one of those encounters? With someone you'd hoped never to see again? When, all of a sudden, it's too late and they're coming straight for you? Yeah? Me, too. Even in a city the size of New York it happens. Just you, them, and an empty street filled to choking on the past. It's like your number's come up in the lottery of debacles.

I'd like to flip on the "Occupied" sign and peel out of there. But the line of cabs is all bunched up, and I'm trapped, and then it's too late. They don't hail me. It's more like they jump me. A hooligan coming at me from either side. I act busy, popping the trunk and loading their bags. They're heavy.

They have no reason to expect to run into me on the east coast. And it's been a while. I try to keep my distance and my back turned as they get in.

"Where to?"

"Uptown. 110th and Amsterdam."

"You got it."

I tilt the rearview mirror so I can't see them and, more crucially, they can't see me. No use letting them study me on the ride uptown. I hunch over and drive. I don't expect to hear anything of interest, these fellows being laconic types themselves.

I'm plenty worried they're gonna recognize me. I've got that gun under the seat, but there's two of them and they're sitting behind me. Who wants to get in a gunfight at work? I'm just tryin' to make a livin' here.

Poochie doesn't even need a gun. His fists are like brickbats. That's how he got his start. He used to be a street fighter for money. He'd take on all-comers. Even professional boxers. And he laid 'em all out. Big Department heard tell and brought him in.

I close the window between us to make it clear I don't want to be disturbed. It doesn't work. Around 14th and Broadway comes some hammering on the glass partition. They're trying to get my attention, authoritative-like. Without turning around, I open the little window and Finnbar squawks at me to pull over. His voice is strangled. He sounds parched.

When I stop, he climbs out and makes a beeline for a liquor store. The meter's running, but what do they care? They're not planning to pay me anyway. It's not their style. He returns soon enough carrying a fifth of something in a brown paper bag and a case of beer. Poochie says to him: "Don't look so surprised. He's still here." I hear them laugh and crack a couple beers before I shut the window again, this time, I hope, for good.

A few blocks later as we're approaching the Garment District, there comes more rapping. I open the slot and Poochie tells me to pull over and pop the trunk. This I do. He says they'll be right back. He grabs their duffel bags from the trunk and heads toward the door of some fur manufacturer.

A few minutes later he comes back in high spirits. He must have sold whatever they had in those duffel bags. They seem relieved to be rid of them.

All I get by way of explanation is Poochie saying: "Well, well, he's still right here. Okay, buddy, let 'er rip." Traffic is light this time of night, and I barrel uptown.

My hearing's sharp enough that I can hear what's said behind me, even with the window shut. My passengers invariably think I can't possibly make out what they're saying. Their false sense of security is nice, up to a point. It's relaxing.

To my surprise, these two do indulge in a little chit-chat on our way uptown. For instance, I learn the ship that brought them back to New York came by way of the Panama Canal. Finnbar can't help but complain that the humidity in New York is practically as bad as it was in Panama.

Poochie readily admits New York's a jungle. Makes me think they had animal skins in those duffel bags. Some big cats they bought on the black market, pumas or lynx or leopards.

Or maybe they had something even more exotic, like rolls of snakeskins. I hear they have anacondas so big down there they can swallow a deer whole, after which they close their eyes and settle in for a six-month siesta to dream about their next big score. You can make a lot of handbags out of a thirty-foot-long snake, if it doesn't swallow you first.

Poochie directs me to an auto repair shop on 110th, in an old Irish neighborhood. When I tell him that'll be $7.50, he laughs and says:

"Why don't you come in and have a drink?"

Then I hear one of them cock a pistol and I say, "Sure."

They march me into the repair shop and have me take a seat on a bent, light green folding chair. To my surprise, they actually do offer me a beer. The place reeks of oil.

"You think I didn't recognize you, Johnny Boy? Now that we're back in town, we're looking for something to do. Maybe the fur factory we stopped at is worth a go."

"I'm just a taxi driver these days, Poochie."

"Where can I find you, in case we need a wheelman?"

"The number's on the side of the cab."

"Can you still see in the dark, Johnny Boy?"

"As well as the next fellow."

"Not better?"

"Not anymore. I got it knocked out of me."

"You shoulda seen this guy drive with the lights off," Poochie says to Finnbar. "Now that I think about it, I might need a gopher, too, to tunnel into that place."

I sip some beer to keep from making it obvious how much I'm sweating my latest job interview. He gets the number off the taxi and gives me a card for the auto shop, in case I hear of anything juicy. It's clear he expects me to call sometime soon, or else, and that it better be good. I tell him I'll keep my ears open. The kiss-off. Anything to get out of there.

What's weird is soon I'll be working for a tannery. And there's nothing simpler than an inside job. But, again, it depends on the job.

CHAPTER 34

THE BUM'S RUSH

The $22.50 Man

When I go into work on Monday morning, I get some bad news. My boss calls me into his office and tells me the guys downtown have decided to yank me, there and then. My cover's blown and so they can't really use me anymore. This is bad. I could use the $22.50 a week. They still want to debrief me, apparently, so I go downtown to headquarters. I tell my handler the last things I've overheard. He's interested in what I have to say about driving the fur mogul to Pennsylvania, and how he wanted me to keep it quiet. Then it's over. He stands up and shakes my hand and wishes me the best of luck. The bum's rush.

I don't bother to tell him about Poochie and Finnbar. Better to let sleeping dogs lie. The cops can listen to the tape if they find the time. They won't learn much even if they do. Those two weren't that talkative. Poochie waited to get me into the chop shop before he tipped his hand.

CHAPTER 35

GOLF CART SURVEILLANCE

I go home and tell Ariane the bad news about getting shown the door. It's a blow. Still, I'll find something else soon enough. I hope. I also tell her about giving Poochie a ride, and how he's adamant I do him a favor.

I have another idea and figure I'll go back to the guys at headquarters and run it by them. Maybe they'll take me up on it. Ariane makes me a Manhattan and we toast to—what else? Tomorrow and tomorrow and tomorrow.

The next morning, I head uptown and go in to see the boys in blue. I didn't arrange an appointment, so they make me sit around for a while before they give me five minutes with the boss.

"All right, LeFouet, what's this idea you want to wow me with?"

"I've got another place where we can do some listening and I think we'll uncover all sorts of leads."

"Go on."

"I once had a job as a golf caddie and those golfers make a big deal about being able to talk freely when they're golfing. Who knows what kind of schemes they're discussing?"

"Huh."

"Yeah, we could hook up one of those recording devices to their golf bag, or their golf cart. I bet we'd learn more than we learn eavesdropping in taxis."

"You might be on to something."

"Think of the people who golf. Rich people. Businessmen. Politicians. Celebrities."

"And so, we listen to their private conversations when they think they're all alone?"

"Exactly. Like we do with the cabs."

"What would you do?"

"I'd plant the recorders. Steer them to the right cart. Retrieve them afterwards. That kind of thing."

"I don't see it."

"Why not?"

"Nah. No way."

"Why?"

"The mayor loves golf. He never loses. He'd rip my head off if he heard we were spying on him and his golf buddies. Golf is like sacred to the guy."

"But…"

"I don't want to hear another word about this. If I do, I'll have your hide."

On my way home, it's hot as blazes and I find myself suffering from an acute thirst. In a dark corner of some mostly forgotten bar, left alone for a change, I take the time to drink and think. How am I going to make a buck? I can try another cab company. Or maybe business is picking up down on Wall Street. Eventually, after five or six beers, I come up with another idea.

I'm going to get my own damn recorder. Fuck those guys. I'm going to find out where the mayor golfs. I'm going to bribe one of the golf cart guys to help me. And I'm going to hide a recorder in his cart the next time he plays golf with Racker. After their carefree, profane, unsuspecting round, I'm going to pay off the cart kid and get that tape. That's it! I'm going to become a fucking freelancer! These cops don't know what a great opportunity this is. All the fat cats who think they're alone when they're out on the links, that they can talk freely, make all their crooked deals and shit. They're in for a big surprise. Done right, I'm gonna make a fortune on golf carts wired for sound.

In the clear light of day the next morning, suitably hungover, I concede it's a less-than-certain scam. At best, it has to be considered speculative.

CHAPTER 36

FURRIER AND FURRIER

Losing that $22.50 job hurts my long-range financial plans, like us paying rent month after next. I figure I'll land another cabbie gig, but word travels. Not everybody loves the deputy. In fact, no one likes police plants or informers or spies. You're persona non grata. It appears I've been blacklisted. They're afraid I'll turn them in, for whatever BS they're up to. I make them nervous. In short, no one wants me around. I could swear I've retired, but why would they believe me?

I go back to chasing film work. I give film labs a try. Nothing doing. I try the big film companies. No openings. It's such a huge town. If you see a job opening, it takes you all day to get there, fill out the paperwork, and come home empty-handed. Ten thousand guys are desperate to beat you out for the crummiest job. Ariane tries to keep my spirits up but it's obvious she's worried, too. She's not raking it in selling books, but at least she still has a job.

Then I come across a card in my wallet for one Jacob Racker—furrier, tanner, and as I'm well aware, bon vivant. I'll call him. I'll tell him I'd like to take him up on his offer to work in his fur operation. If the offer's still good. It was only a couple weeks ago that I drove him all the way to Wellsboro, Pennsylvania. (Remember me? The cabbie with all the French gastronomy? We

feasted for two hundred miles together.) I talk it over with Ariane and she thinks maybe I should give it a shot, why not? It's something, but it's awfully far away. It's hard keeping your head above water these days.

That afternoon, since Ariane's not opposed, I give Jacob Racker a call. He remembers me, sure enough, and thankfully he says his job offer still stands. He wants to know when I can start. I say tomorrow. He wants to know if I'd be willing to drive the midnight shift. I say I am, that in fact it's my specialty.

The next evening, I take the train from Penn Station to Racker's tannery in Wellsboro, Pennsylvania. The Big Overcoat isn't there, but the foreman has instructions on how he's to use my services. The place is running round-the-clock and I'm going to be one of the company's truck drivers. This certainly makes sense to me. There's a lot of hauling required in the manufacture of leather goods apparently.

Before handing me the keys, the foreman gives me the grand tannery tour. The place sprawls across several workrooms. The actual tanning takes place in the largest work areas. These are dark, steamy rooms with metal roofs and big windows flung open for ventilation. Guys are hard at work curing skins. The process takes several days of soaking raw skins in huge chemical baths to turn them into leather. One room is devoted to cowhides that will eventually be turned into everything from shoe leather to leather jackets. Another is devoted to the more delicate operation of preparing furs—raccoon mainly—to be used for fur coats.

When I ask the foreman what goes into the tanning

baths, he shows me other storage rooms. One houses drums of chemicals. Another is filled with cordwood, a chipper, and piles of wood chips. It's all hemlock. "You need hemlock for tanning and the woods around this part of Pennsylvania are filled with hemlock trees. Hemlock is the essential ingredient. That's why the tannery is located here. This part of the state is full of tanneries."

The last storage room he shows me, weirdly enough, is stocked with pigeon shit. I've never seen a place that was so full of shit. Lime, it turns out, is also a vital ingredient in the tanning process. No wonder the place reeks. Racker's got a couple guys who know where to find bird droppings in bulk. On bridges or statues or something. And there's not a lot of competition for it, seeing most people don't recognize the value. These scavengers have got a steady business going in dung mongering. The whole shebang is a hunting and gathering operation. The whole setup could be straight out of the Middle Ages.

It's interesting. Probably worth filming.

The foreman has some good news for me, which is that Racker has told him that my assignment is to drive back and forth to Manhattan. I'll haul skins from the slaughterhouses in the Meatpacking District on the Lower West Side of Manhattan to the tannery in Pennsylvania. On the return trip to New York, I'll transport cured leather and furs to the Garment District to be cut and sewn. They make all sorts of stuff, even saddles and bridles for the horses that clip-clop tourists around Central Park. But their steadiest work is stamping out shoe leather for the New York Police Department.

Out back of the factory are pens and row upon row

of cages filled with raccoons and mink and rabbits. Boy, was that a sad sight. I even thought I spotted a stray cat in there! The foreman offers to show me their slaughterhouse—which he warns me is a bloody shambles. It's right there on the premises, complete with butchers and skinners, but I wave him off. Some other time. Maybe never.

The guy gives me some last good news. All I have to do today is deliver a load to the Garment District. Then tomorrow night I'll start the round trips by picking up the raw skins in the Meatpacking District and bringing them to Wellsboro. He tells me to park the truck in the sweatshop lot when I deliver the leather to the Garment District. Before he sends me off, he mutters that Racker must really have taken a shine to me. It usually takes years to work up from being a dredger to being a driver. I let it slide. Talking too much is for dopes.

So how about that? No more driving two hundred miles around the Five Boroughs, eight hours a day, grabbing fares here, ditching them there. Now I'll just do one eight-hour round trip a day. A bit like my moonless midnight whiskey runs... but with the headlights on. You might think this sounds like a tedious, dull, flat, tired, banal kind of life. So what? What do you want from me? It's the Depression. You hold on for dear life if you're lucky enough to find a job. It didn't turn out to be dull enough, though—not by a long stretch.

My maiden trip I steer a truckload of newly cured leather to the Garment District. The beauty of working the midnight shift is that I get to navigate the streets of New York City when most people are asleep. It would be a lot trickier if I were coming and going midday. The truck's nothing special but I get the hang of it and I'm back in business.

The place where the leather is fashioned into clothes and shoes is huge and it's running full-bore in the wee hours of the night. Half of the operation is automated. The other relies on cobblers working by hand. In one room dozens of cobblers are bent over their work sewing. In another the sound is maddening of the stamping machines cutting out leather soles for different sized shoes. Cops in New York have to be over five-six and so Racker isn't trying to make shoes for everyone. The place is channeled with conveyor belts carrying stacks of cut soles to the seamstresses to sew to the uppers. They've got their work cut out for them. Now the expression makes sense.

Ariane is asleep herself when I climb into bed. Our schedules are going to be screwed up, but we'll be able to have dinner together. She wakes up for a moment and gives me a kiss.

"What time is it?"

"Around 8:00 a.m."

"Are you already done?"

"For today. Tomorrow's my first full day."

"What's that smell?"

"Do I smell?"

"Do you ever," Ariane murmurs.

"I should have showered."

"Go."

"I'll wash. I'll be back in a minute. I don't know why I didn't think of it."

The $22.50 Man

"Bye."

As I wash myself in our cramped little shower, I think about this new business I'm in and how lucky I am to have Ariane.

CHAPTER 37

GRAVEYARD SHIFT

I've worked dark nights before. This is nothing new to me, but I admit it's been a few years. When I reach Wellsboro, Pennsylvania, with a truck full of raw animal skins, I see how dead things are at Racker's factory in the dead of night. There's only a skeleton crew, which I guess is appropriate. Other men haunting the place are lifers. This is what they're going to be doing until they retire or keel over. They're the invisible citizens of the world—asleep during the day, going through the motions all night. The obverse life, as if they were working on the dark side of the moon. Only their wife and kids even know they exist, if they have any. I discover that some of them don't mind their exile from the rest of the world. The whole place slows down, and guys find ways to pass the time.

One fellow seems to be able to sleep standing up. A young black guy who's working his way through college, always has a book he's reading. An old-timer brings a BB gun to work and practices target shooting when no one's around, none of the supervisors anyway. He works in an isolated part of the tannery. I come upon him one night when I'm waiting for my leather shipment to be ready to load. He's seated on a crate with an empty beer can set up about twenty feet away from him. He doesn't seem at all concerned that I've caught him at it. He tells me not to mind his zip gun, he ain't gonna hurt me. Then he takes aim at that beer can and pulls the trigger. He sends it flipping through the air. The can makes more noise when it lands than the gun did. Maybe he's put some sort of silencer on it. He climbs to his feet, hobbles over to retrieve the can, and sets it back up.

"Now I'm showin' off," he says, and gives me a little smile.

"Nice shot," I say.

"I've had time to practice. Eighteen years."

"I just started. Driving a truck."

"Name's Traumer," he says, introducing himself.

"John. Nice to meet you."

"Likewise. Give me a bit more warning next time you pop in. Wouldn't want to, you know, wing you."

"Me either. I won't sneak up on you. I'll knock or cough or something."

"Be sure to talk to the union rep. All the truckers are teamsters."

"What's his name?"

"Aspellino. Don't make him come lookin' for you."

"I won't."

I would have thought the foreman would have mentioned the union to me. It kind of goes without saying, I guess. I'll join.

The same crazy guy who was cackling to himself the first time I came apparently works the midnight shift, too. He's a dredger, shoving skins into the hemlock bath, agitating them every few minutes, before dredging them out when they're cured. Inhaling those fumes must be affecting his brain. When Traumer and I are talking, he comes hustling past. No one says anything and then he's gone again. I turn back to the old-timer, and he raises his eyebrows, giving the dredger a vote of little confidence.

"What's up with him? I noticed him the first time I was here."

"The boss's nephew. Part of the wife's family," says Traumer.

"Seems kinda nutty," I say quietly.

"I'd have as little to do with him as you can," he says. "He's unpredictable."

"Good to know."

"This place uses all sorts of chemicals. I think he's found something he likes, helps him get through his shift. It strikes me he's sniffing himself halfway mad. I try not to take any notice of him, but it's hard."

"How long's he been working here?"

"A couple of years."

"You ever had a run-in with him?"

"No, but some of the other crew have. If he weren't family, he'd have been sacked months ago."

"What's his name?"

"We call him Brick. For goldbrick. I think his real name's Otis."

"Well, those skins are probably ready for loading. Better shove off. Nice talking to you, Traumer."

"So long."

CHAPTER 38

CAT NAPPING

Home is where the warm is. Too warm now. I no like.
My coat is hot, so hot. Stay outside, out and about. Can't outrun my coat. Want to lick a puddle. Where's some wet? What's that with trees over there? I hear water across the quiet and dark.
Creep, creep. Watch for rats. Watch for black-masked attackers diving out of stink bins.
I smell pigeons. They're not like us. They never clean up after themselves. Always painting the town white.
Whoa! I see a tall cat moving near a little pond of wet. I'm curious! Creep and lurk. What's it do? Why the big do-do? Scraping dried, lumpy pigeon plop in the middle of the dark?
Meow, the thirst! So hot. I creep up to the little wet, slinking in the dark. The tall cat comes to me slowly. It meows to me. I keep my eyes on it and lick up some wet, quick quick.

Not quick enough. The tall cat grabs me by the scruff of the neck. I'm dangling. I fight and flail. It won't let go. It throws me in a room-that-goes and whambam slams the door.

"Meow," I meow. "Meow! I'm being catnapped!"

Behind the room-that-goes I hear bang, scrape, clang, more bang, more slam. When the tall cat opens another door, I'm ready and try to bolt out, but the tall cat is big and rough, blocks me, shoves me back.

The tall cat smells of big stink. I don't like. It does things and the room-that-goes screeches and shivers all over like a wet dog. Trees slide by outside.

The tall cat meows to me. It gives me a bite of food. I like. I'm scared. I smell a rat and pigeons. I'm a scaredy. How will I find my tall cats? How will I find my bowls? Home is where the icebox is. And my tall cats. The one-who-feeds and the one-who-pets.

There's music. That's nice. I'm edgy and sleepy. I fall asleep on the floor, on top of the bump bump and grinding gears.

CHAPTER 39

TURPITUDE

Quick. No one's on the floor.

Duck in back, my secret. My office. The skins ain't goin' no place. They ain't jumpin' outta the bath and swimmin' around. They're workin' and I'm workin' at restin'. Hehehehe. Quick quick, the Turpy, out with the Turpy. Hand's shakin'. Is that new? When'd my hand start shakin'? Unscrew it. Almost dropped the cap. Careful. I call it that, Turpy, Turpyturp, cuz it's resiny smellin' like turpentine. The stuff you clean your paintbrush with. One little whiff cleans the ol' brush, don't it? It do. But it ain't pine. It's the good stuff, hemlock. Ohhhhhhh. Here it comes. Ohhhhhh. Why can't I take a huge whiff like I used to? Bet I'm turnin' my lungs to leather. Hope not. Someday they'll use 'em to make snowshoes. Hehehehe. I'm walkin' around with a pair of snowshoes in my chest. When winter comes, I'm set I bet, you bet I'm set.

They don't know I do the whiff back here. They

think I'm takin' a siesta. Lick it. Ohhhhhh. Comes it comes. The earthquake numbs. The whole place reeks of hemlock. Everybody's whiffin' turpytine, swimming' in it. Night and steam clouds and fog. Fumey chemicals. That's the one thing I like workin' here. If they told me to wear a mask I'd tell 'em to shove it. Still it's a nightmare this place. Uncle Rack Rack Racker. Uncle Racket. I'm supposed to appreciate it, him givin' me a job in his tannery. As a dredger. This place is a pit. We're gettin' slaughtered. Owner first, workers and animals last. Uncle Racker wants to see me embalmed.

Auntie hates him and his fat guts. I heard her complainin' to Ma plenty. This is his idea of revenge. Such a smart guy. Actin' like he's lendin' the helpin' hand. A big fat hand to shove my head under. When I'm good and cured (that's a good one, cured!) inside and out, hope they stuff me and prop me up in a corner of the tannery. I'll be truly cured. Hehehehe. Here's what we think of neppytism. Here stands Goldbrick Otis, nephew of the boss, Jacob Racker. His kith 'n kin. His bones and skin. His useless nephew. Phewwww. Lick it. Ohhhhhh. Lights and waves. Hot and ohhhhhh. Just lie. Lie. Shaking. Floor's cool on my cheek. Here comes the quake. Numb. I'm lyin' in a snowbank. Ohhhhh. Hot and prickly and cool. Lights and waves and shaky heat and waves and colorlight and shakewaves and colorheat and blindingcold. Creepin' risin' from my boots numbin' num num.

Ohhhhhh. Ohhhhhh. Ohhhhhh. Numbing. Numb. Number. Numbest. Numbskull.

CHAPTER 40

THOSE WHO FEED

There are two kinds of tall cats. Those who feed and those who don't. That's something I've learned in my lives. Those who put you in cages and those who let you out. Those who put me out at night and those who let me in. Where'd he go? The new tall-cat-who-feeds? Maybe he's getting me something. I hope. The second I see him, I'm yowling right up to him. Until he feeds. Sometimes he feeds right away. When he's good. Sometimes I have to yowl and yowl. When he's dumb. Or deaf. Sometimes I nip him on the ankle. When he ignores. When he's bad. He's learning. Sometimes he forgets and I have to remind. These fangs remind. And these claws. Remind him what's what. Remind him who's who. Always be closing in on the new cat-who-feeds.

What's that smell? I smell a smell. Follow. Follow. I smell a smell. I smell a rat!

There, there, over there. Behind those boxes. Beds for

me? Beds for litter? Where's the rat? Squeeze through. My whiskers fit and I fit. Night back here. Still I see. Be quiet now, quiet now. Where's the rat? Creep quietly. Step softly. What's this? A tall cat lying down. Smells like a rat. Poor tall cat. Is it sleeping? I yowl. Nothing. Touch it with my cool nose. It's cold. It smells like a rat. Push it with my head. It ignores. Nip it. It completely ignores. It's wet sticky in here. The tall cat needs help. There are those who are warm and those who are cold. The quick and the dead.

I cry, "Yowl!"

My paws feel sticky. I hear someone. I'm scared. I'm bolting scrambling leaping running, leaving a skidding, skating trail of bloody paw prints.

There are two kinds of tall cats. Scary tall cats and *my* tall cats. Sometimes one of *my* tall cats smells just like this cold, wet, smelly, sticky place. I'm curious. Is *he* here somewhere?

CHAPTER 41

DEATH IN THE TANNERY

I was thinking about how little patience I have for people who are clearly addled in the brain and how I would try to avoid Otis or Brick or whatever his name is. Tonight, when I pull into Wellsboro, I learn someone's hit him with a lily. The guy's been murdered. Shot. They found him by following some bloody paw prints. A regular primrose path.

When I walk inside, guys are standing around smoking, talking, waiting for the police to arrive. The undertakers have already bundled up the corpse and taken it to the coroner's, presumably for an autopsy. The floor's still wet as if someone just mopped up the blood. The place has ground to a standstill. Everyone's holding a wake without the festivities. Finally, one of the supervisors tells us to quit goldbricking and get back to work. Nothing we can do for the guy, he says. Otis is dead as the poor brutes in the shambles.

As inconspicuously as possible I look these guys over, wondering if any of them pulled the trigger. These are leathery characters themselves. No one heard anything. They say the deceased was cold as the cement floor when they found him there stashed back of a bunch of boxes. If the shooter stuffed him back there, it wasn't the perfect hiding place. Not like a proper grave in the depths of a dark wood.

We're all lost in thought as we go back to our business. From my few encounters with Otis, I figure he must have made his share of enemies. I sound out one of the tanners as we load my truck with bundles of freshly cured leather bound for the Garment District in NYC.

"Poor guy," I say. "Young."

"I guess. He ain't gonna be missed," the guy helping me says. "Let the idiot rest in peace. From day one he was a shirker. If he didn't have pull with the boss, he'd have been fired day two."

"He'd still be walking the Earth if they'd fired him," I say.

"Yeah, maybe. It's been obvious for months he was strung out. Laughing for no reason, getting all pissed over union stuff that had nothing to do with him, always doing a half-assed job."

"He seemed loony," I say.

"Maybe he was."

"Could he have committed suicide?"

"They didn't find a gun. Just him."

"Maybe somebody pocketed the gun."

"Maybe, but I don't see why they would. Everyone knows you let murder weapons lie."

"Any idea when he got plugged?"

"He was here working last night. I remember seeing him. He didn't show up for work tonight and the shift boss was pretty ticked off. Then they found him, cold."

"Sounds like last night was his last," I say.

"Yeah."

"Where'd he get it?"

"Right in the temple. Bingo. Killed him like that."

"Terrible."

"Yeah."

"You might have thought it was suicide, except for no gun."

"They forced one of the butchers to clean it up," he says. "He wasn't happy about it, but he said he'd seen worse."

"He probably has."

"Like every day."

"Except, you know."

"Yeah."

"Well, thanks for the hand with this," I say. "I'm off."

"Okay, pal. Watch out for deer."

As I'm motoring toward Manhattan, a police car passes, lights flashing, heading the opposite direction, going to investigate matters.

When the killer plugged Otis, he was dead to the world. He didn't see it coming or know what hit him or even feel a thing. There's some dumb luck for you. The man who knew too little.

CHAPTER 42

INTERROGATION

The next night I arrive in Wellsboro and the supervisor tells me the police want to talk to me. No one likes to hear that kind of repartee. I follow him into his office and there sits a cop, talking to one of the other guys. I'm told to wait outside, he'll get to me. I always spend about an hour at the tannery while we unload the skins that I'm bringing from the Meatpacking District and load the cured leather that I deliver to the Garment District. There's no real urgency. I can wait. It gives me a moment to do a little thought collecting. Let's see. I don't know anything about anything. I didn't see Otis the Goldbrick get shot and I wasn't on the spot when they found him. Still, I guess the cops are trying to be thorough, taking statements from everyone on the midnight shift.

I'm mulling this over when the office door opens and the cop waves me in.

"You're John Laughaway?"

"LeFouet. That's right."
"That's French, isn't it?"
"That's right."
"Are you from France originally?"
"Montreal."
"Been working here long?"
"Didn't the foreman tell you?"
"How 'bout you tell me."
"I started a couple months ago."
"What did you do before you started in on this racket?"
"I was a taxi driver in New York."
"Which outfit?"
"Yellow Cab."
"Why'd you quit?"
"I got tired of all the company."
"Enjoy the graveyard shift?"
"It pays the bills."
"Fair enough. What can you tell me about your deceased coworker, Otis?"
"Just what I observed the few times I crossed paths with him. He was odd. I frankly thought he was crazy or high on something. The first time I met him he came out from behind some stuff piled in a corner, out of the dark, kind of talking and laughing to himself. I had the impression he'd been sleeping back there."
"Did you hear anything the night he was killed?"
"What night was that?"
"We think it was two nights ago, midnight shift—the night before they found him."
"No, I didn't hear anything."
"See anything?"

"No. I usually only spend forty-five minutes or an hour here the nights I work, just the time it takes to unload skins from the city and load leather for the return trip. I'm not here all night. I usually get here around 3:00 a.m. and am back on the road by 4:00 a.m. It's four hours each way."

"Do you know if Otis had any enemies?"

"No."

"You ever see any guns around here?"

"No. And I'm not in the habit of frisking people."

"Do you own a gun?"

"Me? No. What kind of gun was it?"

"I can't talk about that. We're still actively investigating."

"I get it."

"My job is to ask questions, not answer them. Did you hear anyone bad-mouthing the victim?"

"No."

"Was he in the union?"

"I was told everyone had to join the union. But I don't know about him. I heard he was the owner's nephew."

"Any talk about striking?"

"Who knows? I just load my truck and take off again. I'm not a lifer here."

As I motor back to Manhattan, I replay my conversation with the investigator. Unfortunately, to be honest, I had seen a gun at the tannery. Traumer had that pastime, the BB gun. I didn't want to get him in trouble. He doesn't strike me as the murderous type, not by a long shot. I met some gangsters and gunmen and hooligans during Prohibition, murderous guys like Poochie. I even worked with them. I know the type. If I start blabbing about the old guy's hobby, he'll lose his job. And for what? To shove a poor guy into the breadlines? Or some federal penitentiary? Sadly, someone else let the cat out of the bag. They arrest the old guy on suspicion of murder.

CHAPTER 43

TAP OF THE MORNING

After I deliver the load of leather to the Garment District, I'm feeling thirsty and instead of going home, I drop into a dingy little bar that caters to guys like me getting off the midnight shift in the morning. Who says you can't have a beer before noon? The night is young. It's just going into extra innings.

I've hardly had time to ascertain if my pint's cold and wet when a guy sits down next to me, gives me a sidelong look, and starts talking quietly. He wants to know if I'd be interested in going back undercover. Do I want my old job back, you know, as a $22.50 man?

"The guy who grilled you tonight ran your name and found out you used to work for us."

"And?"

"He thinks you might be able to help us catch the guy who murdered Racker's nephew."

"What do you want me to do?"

"Keep your eyes and ears open when you're there. And let us know what you learn."

"Fair enough. What else?"

"It so happens we're also interested in Racker himself. We understand you became friendly with him."

"Not that friendly. But it's a pretty long trip to Wellsboro, Pennsylvania. He liked me well enough to hire me."

"We think he's bribing our fine, upstanding public servants. He landed the latest NYPD shoe contract, even though he seems to have put in the highest bid. And the mayor's wife's wearing a new mink coat."

"Probably said he'd deliver the highest quality leather."

"His nephew isn't the first guy to die there in recent memory. Another guy 'accidentally' drowned in a tanning bath a few months back. When the police investigated, no one knew a thing. They seemed to think he must have slipped. He'd practically turned to leather himself by the time they found him."

"Poor guy."

"He didn't even work there. He just got deep-sixed there."

"Huh."

"We're trying to catch the culprit but no one will talk. Maybe you'll have better luck. You're already part of their operation."

"It's an unhealthy environment, for sure. I'm nuts to frequent the place. I hate to ask, but how much will I make?"

"$22.50 a week."

"Make it $25. I'm practically an old pro at this point."

"I got zero discretion. $22.50 men make $22.50. It's

right there in the job title."

"You could hire me as a $25 man."

"Sorry, Laughaway. Though, I've got some good news for you. Racker is offering a reward for catching his nephew's killer."

"How much?"

"$1,000."

"Fine, it's a deal. But skip issuing me an ID. That was a blunder."

"I heard."

"Should I call you if I learn something?"

"Fitzpatrick's still your contact, Tenth Precinct. If you need a wire, he'll help you out."

I'll have to keep my wits about me. It's not easy to be on the alert, and nonchalant, all at the same time. When I get home, Ariane is just climbing out of bed. She's expected at her bookstore in a couple hours.

"I liked it better when you worked regular hours, Jean-Yves. I miss you."

"I'm working on a new angle, Ariane. I'm not going to be doing this much longer."

"What angle? Do you have a new job in the works?"

"I'm not supposed to talk about it. It's top secret," I say. "I'm a $22.50 man again."

"I've been holding off buying some necessities. That $22.50 will come in handy. But I want to see more of you, too!"

"The police have given me a new case to work on. With a big reward."

"How much?"

"A thousand bucks."

"Wow."

"If I figure it out, we'll be in the gravy. Maybe we can even take a little vacation."

"Wonderful," Ariane says. She looks tired. It's draining, this life of ours.

"Maybe we could take that trip to France to visit your parents."

"Yes! I'd love that."

"I would, too. Especially with you."

"Where's Vince?"

"I was going to tell you. I haven't seen him all day. I hope he's just on one of his adventures."

"I hope one of the neighbors hasn't 'adopted' him."

CHAPTER 44

LOTTA FUN

When Ariane and I think about who can help me with my side scam, we both realize at the same instant who the perfect person is: "Lotta!" I get her on the phone and fill her in on how she can help. Lotta readily admits she needs a new job and thinks I'm on to something. I assure her it'll be duck soup. Later that morning, she calls her former employer, Jacob Racker.

"Racker here."

"Hello, Mr. Racker, I don't know if you remember me. Lotta? I worked for you as a maid…?"

"Lotta? Yes, I remember you. You left in a big hurry! But we don't need to talk about that. Why are you calling? What can I do for you?"

"Oh, thank you. Yes, I was hoping you could do something for me."

"You're a funny girl. I could have helped you right here."

"Oh, you know, I got kinda spooked working as your servant."

"That's too bad. I'm sorry about all that."

"But I liked you, Mr. Racker. And you seemed to like me."

"Yes, I did. Except when you came between me and my breakfast. But that wasn't cause for firing you. I wasn't going to let you go," he says.

"Well, that's the thing. I was wondering if you could help me find another position somehow?"

"I don't know anyone who needs a maid."

"That's no problem. What I was wondering is if you might be able to get me a little job at your golf club?"

"At my club?"

"Why not? I love golf meself. And you did make it hard for me to keep working in your home, seeing how crowded it was gettin'."

"Well, Lotta, I'll see what I can do. It would be nice to see you at the club. Give me your number. I'll make a call."

"Oh, aren't you a sweetheart," Lotta says. "Thank you!"

CHAPTER 45

DEADPAN DORA

The Big Overcoat is feeling quite sporty. He's got some nice golf duds on. Domestic tranquility seems to be holding since he's come back home from his retreat to the tannery. His wife, Pandora, is asleep upstairs, and the maid's making breakfast. After his steak and eggs, he'll be off to play golf with the mayor. (He might even see Lotta again at his club!) Who doesn't like a Saturday round of golf on a crisp fall morning?

He should find occasion to deploy his new niblick and his good old mashie. And maybe even his profitable putter. But he's got to be more careful. The last time playing with the mayor almost ended very badly. It makes him feel a bit queasy thinking about it. It makes him hungry and impatient.

"Where's my food, Dora? I'm in a hurry!"

"Coming right up!"

He remembers it with horror. They're on the eighteenth green, and the mayor decides to bet him another $250 that he can't make a five-foot putt. Fifty bucks a foot! It's not a big deal. He's planning to miss on purpose, anyway, so the mayor will "win" some money off him, and he'll stay in his good graces. All kosher, too, according to the chief of police.

But then, unfortunately, the ball for some perverted reason veers the wrong way... toward the cup! For a second it looks like it's going in the damn thing! If he'd made the putt, Racker tells himself he would have had to wave off the bet. But even that wouldn't have rectified the problem of putting more money in the mayor's pocket, ostensibly fairly and all square. The mayor likes to win.

As he's vowing never not to miss a putt like that again, for the sake of his heart, the door to the kitchen swings open and in bustles his maid, Dora, carrying a silver serving tray with coffee, orange juice, and a plate piled high with hash browns, fried eggs, and a New York steak.

As she arranges his breakfast neatly in front of him, he scans the table for the salt mill. It isn't there.

"Dora, could you get me some salt?"

"Oh, sir, I got some bad news," she says. "The saltshaker broke the other day. The porcelain inside cracked and the whole thing got ground up and jammed, and so we got rid of it."

"Oh."

"It could have been dangerous to one's health," she says.

"I don't really care about the saltshaker itself, Dora. I'd just like some salt for my steak and eggs."

"Well, that's the other bad news. The missus doesn't want you overindulging in salt. She specifically ordered me not to buy any."

"What the hell? Oh, never mind! Never mind. I'll survive. That'll be all."

As he waves her off, she calls back over her shoulder: "Orders is orders, Mr. Racker, sir. Enjoy your breakfast."

Why does that maid always have that blank expression? Racker asks himself. She's pretty. There's something not right about her, though she knows her way around a breakfast table. She's impossible to read. Should take up poker. The one and only Deadpan Dora.

After she retreats, and there's no one else around, he reaches discreetly into his wallet, takes out a small package of white powder, tears it open, and quickly sprinkles it on his steak. Then he skewers the steak with his fork, flips it over and salts the other side. Only then he digs in with immense contentment. It takes true gluttony to fill a big overcoat.

What a nice morning it is!

Eating with relish, he's happy to think that maybe she doesn't want him dead, Pandora, the old gal, after all. Look at her, the irascible one. She wants me to take care of myself. She wants to keep me alive. Her trying to ban salt is absurd, I'll bring my own, but the sentiment is kind of sweet. I love salt, but she's being sweet. Imagine that. We're still opposites. Sweet and salty.

CHAPTER 46

A COMEDY OF ERRORS

When you have the kind of pull the Big Overcoat has, things happen fast. Later that morning, he and the mayor arrive at his club for eighteen holes of what can only be described as middling golf, and Lotta is there in the clubhouse to greet them. She's sporting a trim white dress and a genuinely radiant smile. With one phone call, Racker had procured her a job behind the counter in the pro shop. She checks them in, makes sure they have scorecards, and gives them the key to a golf cart. She even promises to bring them a bucket of balls for the practice range.

As Racker and his illustrious guest are securing their clubs to the cart, Lotta floats toward them like a golfer's dream, smiling, looking smashing, bearing a bucket of balls. But, alas, something goes awry. Her foot slips on the cart path and as she goes to regain her balance, a half-dozen balls spill out and begin bouncing crazily toward the two older men. Wanting to impress her with their athleticism and agility, they both do their best to track down the wayward golf balls. Who would have thought that such a cute young lady could unleash such chaos? She, too, hurries to help, but she only makes matters worse, dumping another dozen balls in the process.

When they manage to gather them all back up, Lotta hands them the bucket with the rest of the balls, apologizing and swearing she'll never make such a stupid mistake again.

"You better go back to the shop," says Racker. "Leave the range ball responsibilities to someone else."

"Yes, no, that's a fine idea, sir. I will, I promise. And thank you again," says Lotta. "Have fun out there." Then she leans over toward the Big Overcoat and gives him a peck on the cheek. "For luck!" She gives the mayor a kiss on the cheek, too, laughing a little. "You can use luck, too, right?"

When the two men climb in their golf cart, the mayor gives Racker a long look.

"What the hell?"

"I'm sorry, Mayor. She's new."

"I'm sorry, too. I pulled a muscle in my back trying to scramble after those damn balls."

"She's pretty cute, though, wouldn't you say?"

"Yes, she is," the mayor concedes, finally lightening up a little. "Oh, my back's all right."

"I think she has a soft spot for me," Racker says, leering slightly. "Used to work for me as a maid. She's kissed me before. But I had to let her go. Too cute and clumsy for Pandora."

"Her grace and charm will undoubtedly serve her well here," says the mayor. "What's her name, this beauty?"

"Lotta."

"Well, let's go have a whole lotta fun."

"Yessir!"

"Hope you brought a pocket full of twenties, Jacob. I'm feeling lucky today."

"What do you say we up the ante, Mr. Mayor? I brought fifties. I'm feeling lucky, myself."

CHAPTER 47

DREDGING UP THE PAST

Over the next few nights, I do my best to learn more about the Brick's demise and about the guy they hauled from the tanning bath. People remember seeing Otis at work the night in question, but he disappeared halfway through his shift. The other dredgers complained that they had to pick up the slack, but they said it wasn't out of the ordinary. If the guy was anything, it was undependable. When I talked about it with one of the skinners, he kind of laughed, telling me that at least Otis hadn't made too much of a mess on his way out. In fact, he said he'd seen chinchillas that had bled more than Otis had.

Rumor has it the dead guy they pulled out of the tanning bath had made noises about not joining the union. Why would he have bothered to buck the union? Trying to work as a scab would hardly seem wise or healthy or low-profile. It made no sense, so I rejected that idea. Maybe the guy I talked to was just trying to put a scare into me, the new guy. Another guy flat out contradicted that theory.

"He's thinking of another guy. I heard the dead guy was a sales rep from a rubber company. It's slippery around those tanning baths. He musta slipped."

"Should have watched his step," I can't help but agree.

"Maybe them gumshoes ain't skidproof after all."

When I originally talked to the union rep, Aspellino, he let drop something interesting. He complained in no uncertain terms that Otis had refused to join the union, but that they couldn't get rid of him, because his uncle owned the operation. I assured him I was a big union man myself. I was eager to sign on the dotted line, join the teamsters, and kick in my dues. He told me I had no choice; it was a union shop. I sounded him out about other jobs at the tannery, like dredging. Was that a union job, too?

He said all the jobs were with one union or another. The dredgers were part of the Leather Workers Union. I would have thought they were part of the Haberdashers Union. Is there such a thing? In any event, no union card, no job. With the one glaring exception of Racker's nephew. The Big Overcoat got around it by calling Brick his personal assistant.

During Prohibition, the Bootleggers Union was a looser affiliation. Big Department, Poochie, Finnbar, Granyer, Akihiro. All of them. The Green Gang. They'll lie or take the Fifth before they tell anyone who's in their club. They wouldn't recognize me if I were in the same room with them. How should they know who their driver was? It was dark out. All they ever saw was some dark hat and the back of my head. They have no idea what color the hat was. All hats are black after midnight.

If asked if they could identify my voice at least, they'd be relieved to tell the truth for a change: "The guy wasn't some radio announcer. I never even heard him yawn."

Generally true, all that. I learned early on, if there's anything to talk about, whatever you do, don't talk about it. Comport yourself like the tight-lipped presidents on the greenbacks. Never a word about the company you keep or where you've been.

Still. That was the name they knew me by.

"So, if you had to, how exactly would you describe him?"

"I just told you. There was nothing to know. He was still as an unmarked grave."

I shudder a little thinking back on that dangerous business, smuggling Canadian whiskey into the lower forty-eight.

CHAPTER 48

BAD DOG

There's my old tall cat! There in the dark and the stink. By the big wet. *My* tall cat! I want to rub his hind leg, bump him with my head. The one-who-feeds. When he sees me, he'll free me. He's opening my cage! He meows, "Vince!" Where's he been? What's he been eating? I can't tell. I can't smell him. There's too much stink. So many animals.

Whoa!

A big dark dog! Bad Poochie!! Crouch. Lurk, lurk. It doesn't see me, Vince the Invincible. It's looking at my tall cat. It's about to spring. I know that growl. That means run! Run, tall cat, run! The tall cat doesn't hear. He doesn't turn. He's opening other cages.

The big dog rushes and jumps at my tall cat! They fall by the wet. No! I'm faster than the big dog. I jump all fangs and claws. I bite and scratch. I'm a storm. It howls. It scrambles off my tall cat. It tries to run away and slips

Richard Voorhees

and splashes in the big wet. My friend the tall cat rolls over and jumps up and sees me. He looks at the big dog splashing in the wet. He stares. He picks up a sticky skin and throws it on top of the big dog in the wet. That slows him down. My big cat grabs me up. Why come where we go for?

Outside I see animals behind fences in cages. They stare at us. My tall cat opens one two three four five six seven eight more cages. So fast. The animals run out. I'm scared. He holds me tight. I grab him with my claws. He squeezes me tight. So many animals all run run run. He runs carrying me to the room-that-goes. He shoves me in and jumps in after. The door slams. It roars. I stand next to him and watch.

Other tall cats come outside and stare at all the running animals. They all run around and around. My tall cat moves a stick and turns a wheel and we shake and roar and go go go. The other tall cats get small and go away. My tall cat, the one-who-feeds, opens a window and I smell trees and I see trees run past and I bump jump on the floor. It's moving and roaring.

I try to rub against his leg, but he meows, "No, Vince." He picks me up under my middle and sets me up again next to him. This time I stay. I lie down and look up as the trees fly by. With my hair sticking out like this, like a big tree, I'm as big as that dog. Bigger. And sharper.

"Vince, boy, am I glad to see you. You saved me from that dog. Ariane and I missed you. We were worried."

Finally, the tall cat meows my name. I was wondering "Where's your tongue?"

Time to start purring. Things fly by and fly by. I

look at my tall cat. He looks calm. And wet. He smells like things under the sink. It's dark and things fly by. I'm sleepy. Time for a nap. I'm going to swallow the world with a yawn.

I wake up as the room-that-goes stops. My big cat picks me up and carries me into a bright room full of tall cats in blue.

After I deliver the skins to the Garment District and get paid, I stop by headquarters. Vince and I head up to see Sergeant Fitzpatrick. He points me in the direction of Lieutenant O'Beckett.

"Now what do you got?" O'Beckett snaps. "What's with that mangy thing?"

"I need to talk to toxicology," I say.

"Third floor. Ask for McGillicuddy."

McGillicuddy doesn't give me any guff. He takes Vince off my hands and says he'll see what he can do. I assure Vince I'll wait.

When we get home, my tall cat howls Ariane? The tall-cat-who-pets rushes up to me. She takes me in the little room and splashes me all wet and bubbly. I don't like. Then she wraps me in a blanket and it's warm. She holds me in her arms. Ariane! Where'd my fluff go? I'm skinny, like the animals in cages. The tall cats meow. Vince, Vince, Vince. I smell a smell. A lickable smell. Food!

CHAPTER 49

THE CORONER STUDIES THE CLASSICS

The coroner's report comes back, based on McGillicuddy's analysis. The Brick's death is ruled an accident.

After I brought Vince to headquarters, the toxicologist managed to recover some of Otis the Brick's blood from his paws. When he ran his usual battery of tests, he discovered that the blood sample tested sky-high for hemlock. McGillicuddy sent his finding to the coroner, who confirmed it. Otis didn't die of a gunshot wound at all. He died of hemlock poisoning. The old-timer, Traumer, gets sprung from jail, though it takes them a couple weeks to get around to it.

When I get home, I'm excited to tell Ariane the news. "You know how I've been trying to figure out who killed Racker's nephew? It turns out that when Traumer dinged Otis, through those cardboard boxes, the guy was already dead," I say.

"Wow," says Ariane.

"There was still enough dried blood on Vince's paws to analyze. The coroner ruled that he didn't die from the bullet wound. He poisoned himself."

"Where'd he pick up his poison?"

"The company chemist is distilling hemlock bark all the time for tanning. Otis probably just swiped a little vial's worth whenever he had a chance. No one thought they'd have a problem with that stuff. It's marked 'Poison,' for Christ's sake."

"When he heard it was distilled, he probably thought it was liquor," says Ariane.

"He wasn't thinking straight, hadn't been for months," I say. "Now we know why. He should have studied the classics."

"Or literacy. Then he'd have steered clear. He wouldn't have dared taste it."

"That used to be called a 'fatal draught,'" I say.

"A fatal dram."

"Inhaling it won't kill you immediately but drinking it will," I say. "Even if you're Socrates."

"Especially if you're Socrates," says Ariane.

"Otis died like a true philosopher. Otis and Socrates. Some pair."

"How's the syllogism go?" Ariane wants to know.

"'All men are mortal. Socrates is a man. Therefore, Socrates is mortal.'"

So, Otis died of hemlock poisoning. All Traumer plugged was a dead man's cadaver. The old tanner didn't know Otis was sprawled out back of those boxes. He was simply taking his usual target practice. Just an unfortunate happenstance. You can work in a tannery and die slowly, or you can do it the way Otis did and get it over with.

We still can't believe I found Vince at the tannery or that the bastards were going to turn him into a muff.

CHAPTER 50

CAT HILL

That night I dream Ariane and I are ice-skating across Central Park. Past the section of the park known as Cat Hill. Escaping. There's thick ice underfoot and snow falling. Snow's piling up all over the place. The snow-blanketed trees remind me of the fallen hemlocks in Pennsylvania, all those abandoned white logs stripped of their bark.

The next morning, I give Poochie a call with a plan for knocking over the furrier. Forget tunneling in. I tell him what I overheard, which is exactly when they plan to move the next load of brand-new fur coats. In the dead of night. I tell him I'll be there with my truck to block the alley long enough for them to get the drop on the driver.

CHAPTER 51

FILING MY FINAL REPORT

A taxi waits as I bound up the steps of our brownstone one last time. Our steamer trunk is loaded in, and Ariane is safe in the back seat. I hurry back down the front stoop and leap inside with Vince in his cat carrier. We talk to him to calm him down as the driver pulls away. I tell the cabbie I'll give him a good tip if he gets us to the boat on time.

"Have you got the tickets?" I ask Ariane.

"Yes," she says, "and the passports. I left the key and a check."

"Couldn't be a better time to bid our adieux to Broadway."

En route, I tell Ariane what I learned from my surveillance operation. That Racker paid some fat bribes to the mayor and the chief of police to land the shoe leather contract. That the city was leaning toward going with the man from Rangoon until Racker pulled out his bankroll and began missing more than his share of short putts.

I continue my debriefing, as if I'm talking to myself. Racker's nephew, Otis, wasn't murdered at all. He poisoned himself with hemlock. My hunch had been right. And then, for good measure, I bring up the dead gumshoe salesman. My guess is that Otis did it. He was just out of his mind enough to do such a thing.

I lay all this out loudly, making sure the cabbie can hear everything I say. Ariane tries to get me to speak more quietly, but I keep enunciating. Why? Because I recognize the guy driving the cab. I remember seeing him in passing at the police station.

He's a $22.50 man himself.

Is his cab one of the ones with a tape recorder? Ariane and I are slipping out of town, but I want to pass along the fruits of my detective work. A deal's a deal. Even if it's only for $22.50 a week. Here's my chance. The cabbie's going to have a juicy story to tell if he dares.

When we get out of the cab at dockside, I tell him to hold on, I want to give him the tip I promised him. He laughs and says I've already given him a whopper. That evening it's all splashed across the front page of *The Times*, including pictures of the police chief's wife in ermine and the mayor's wife in a full-length mink coat.

I might have been tempted to give the cabbie the tape of the conversation between the mayor and Racker playing golf, but I'd already sold it to Racker for that $1,000 reward. And some.

Lotta planted my recorder in the golf cart while Racker and the mayor were clambering around trying to corral the balls she spilled. After they finished their round, she retrieved it from their cart and returned it to me. The tape was full of incriminating remarks, as I figured it would be, but just Racker mentioning how Lotta gave him a kiss was enough. He really didn't want the old gal hearing that. He and I simply agreed to tell people it was the $1,000 reward he offered for solving the mystery of the Brick's demise, which I suppose it should have been anyway. The recording just convinced him to make good on his offer. It clinched the deal.

After I read him a few pungent lines over the phone from the transcript I made, he agreed it was worth more than a grand. That's how I sold my first documentary, though it never got broadcast. Lotta said she was going to use her share to pay off the loan sharks in Brooklyn, so maybe she and Dizzy could close that ledger.

A few days later an article in the newspaper chronicles how a robbery in the Garment District got thwarted by the cops. A gang tried to highjack a sixteen-wheeler with enough minks to fill an opera house, but the cops were right there, Johnny-on-the-spot, to smash the fur play or the foul play to smithereens. Some concerned citizen must have tipped them off.

CHAPTER 52

A CIRCLE WITHIN A CIRCLE

We board the ocean liner to Le Havre with our steamer trunk and cat carrier. In our little stateroom, Ariane and I keep our coats on, making sure Vince has water and will be safe. Then we climb the metal stairs to the deck to watch Manhattan disappearing into the distance. The boat's oily wake churns and whirls, looking like an undulating sheet of marbleized paper. Even though I'm loosely tied to the police, it seems prudent to ease out of town. The next thing I know, the flatfeet are going to be chasing after me, the spiller of secrets and liberator of dumb animals. I'd gone from rum-running to front running, and now to this, which I hope will be some fantastically successful outrunning.

When we're back below deck in the privacy of our stateroom, Vince scrambles out of the steamer trunk with Ariane's scroll in his mouth. She shouts at him to drop it. He does, but then he begins biting the jade spindle. I shout at him to stop it. We both shout "Vince!" He knows what we're shouting about.

He scrambles away and leaves the scroll lying there. It looks like he might have broken part of it. Ariane takes it up. Gently she pulls on the end of the jade spindle, the end that seems broken or detached. It comes off in her hand. It's a kind of stopper. The spindle is hollow! We hold it under a lamp. The hollow part contains something. Ariane gets a pair of tweezers out of her toiletries and carefully tries to pull whatever's in there out into the light.

Somewhat surprisingly it slides out without offering much resistance. What's lying in front of us is a tight spool of rice paper. We unroll it. It has visible writing and painting on it. The imagery looks like it could be an illustration from *The Tale of Genji*. Unrolled it's the size of a large postcard, the calligraphy precise, the colors unfaded.

"Can you believe it?" Ariane asks me.

"We'll get it appraised in Paris. It could be worth a lot to the right collector."

"Vince is a good boy."

"He's an art lover!"

Just then comes a knock on the door. Rat-a-tat-tat. It sounds like someone knocking at a three-tap joint in Chinatown. I open the door a crack and a steward's standing there with a bottle of white wine in an ice bucket. In the excitement of finding a scroll within a scroll, I'd forgotten. I arranged this delivery when Ariane was at the ship's railing, looking out to sea. The steward uncorks what turns out to be a bottle of Greek wine, retsina. It tastes like turpentine. Ariane takes a sip and makes a face.

"I'm happy you did as I asked and freed those poor animals," she says.

"Your wish is my command, darling. I would never have found Vince if I hadn't. Imagine. And he wouldn't have saved me from that German shepherd. Or let the genie out of its jade cylinder."

"The Genji from the bottle," says Ariane.

"We might never have known there was anything inside there. The secret inside the mystery entombed in the dented cocktail shaker."

"Such a good boy."

"No doubt. Here, I've got something to read you. You'll see why it's been on my mind."

"By all means," says Ariane. "I'm always reading to you."

I take a slim volume out of my bag. It's Plato's account of the death of Socrates. I find my place and read aloud how the ancients knew twenty-five hundred years ago that hemlock was a poison. (I wouldn't be surprised if the same weren't true of retsina.) I read Plato's description of the trial of Socrates and how he was accused of corrupting the morals of the youth of Athens, encouraging them to question their beliefs, even their faith in the gods. The prosecutors insist on imposing the death penalty. Socrates takes a different tack. He suggests they give him a pension instead. That way he can go on interrogating his fellow Athenians about why they think what they do.

Ariane pours us a second glass of retsina. It doesn't taste as poisonous as the first. I continue reading Plato's account. Socrates is found guilty and is in fact sentenced to death. He submits to the sentence imposed upon him—to drink hemlock.

Plato describes the almost immediate effect of the poison on Socrates, the numbness that began creeping up his legs, how he lay down on the bed in his cell and bore the blow of official injustice.

It's a moving tale. Plato writes that Socrates chose to die as an Athenian citizen, in Athens, rather than flee in the middle of the night as his friends urged him to do. He chose to be subject to the laws and judgment of his beloved city—of beauty and reason, science and doubt, comedy and tragedy, freedom and slavery, Sophocles and Pericles, Euripides, Aristophanes, and radical democracy.

"Now I can tell you what I wished for," Ariane says, "when we pulled our Maraschino cherries apart and I won: I wished for all of this."

"And for our narrow escape," I say.

"At least so far."

"Besides, they're almost done laying train tracks right up to the tannery. In no time, they won't need truck drivers at all."

"So much the better, Jean-Yves."

"Seriously. What a shambles! Nothing like honorable everyday medieval toil."

"Can you believe we found the poet's scroll, and the scroll within the scroll?"

"In our dented cocktail shaker," I say.

"*Oui.*"

"And you're not done, right?" I ask. "There's still more to unravel."

"There's more," says Ariane.

"Vince, from now on you be a good boy!" I shout, pretending to speak his lingo.

"I have a new translation," Ariane says. "Would you like to hear it?"

"Of course."

Ariane takes out her notebook and begins to read:

"When I think back,
I realize I've devoted precious
days and hours distilling this story,
as if I were a salt burner
channeling the sea,
boiling it over
my candle's valiant,
self-devouring flame.
And now, as you see,
all that's left is salt and steam.
Oceans of possibilities
brought me to this and you."

Then Ariane and I kiss one another as if we mean it and we do.

The End

THE AUTHOR

Richard Voorhees is the author of several novels, including Book One of The Genji Trilogy—*Shooting Genji; A Little Too Rambunctious;* and, *The Royal and Ancient Golf Curse;* screenplays; and *Old Pros (A Literary Dictionary of the World's Oldest Professions).* His film, *Proust + Vermeer*, premiered at the De Young Museum in San Francisco. He studied English at Dartmouth College and Film Theory at the University of Paris III.

He's a Seattle native. www.rgvoorhees.com.

WHAT THE CRITICS ARE SAYING ABOUT
Shooting Genji
Book One of the Genji Trilogy

In this comic novel, a front-runner for gangsters leaves New York for Hollywood, where he becomes involved in filming a 1,000-year-old Japanese book.

Following the 1929 stock market crash, Jean-Yves LeFouet, the French-Canadian who narrates this engaging tale, figures it's time to leave town: His boss, who was involved in a shady bunco scam, has just been thrown out of a high window by angry investors. Scamming isn't Jean-Yves' preference; "something of a drifter," he's fallen into jobs like rumrunning. "I love books and reading and the life of the mind and all that, but smuggling booze pays considerably better," he says. So when he hightails it for California, it's not long before he gets a job running errands, caddying and chauffeuring for a small-time film producer. Englishman Charles Blaine Granyer ("Chilblain" to Cambridge pals) wants to adapt *The Tale of Genji*, written by Japanese noblewoman Murasaki Shikibu in the 11th century, into an erotic film.

Jean-Yves juggles his job, his growing interest in a lovely haiku-writing bookseller and various underworld intrusions—including the return of "Big Department," the quarter-ton, 6-foot-7-inch overlord of his New York days. Upton Sinclair, Louise Brooks and Fritz Lang all make appearances as well. Voorhees (*The World's Oldest Professions*, 2013, etc.) has written what is very much a fun, champagne-fueled romp, but the book is well-grounded in realistic details and offers many thoughtful, witty observations from poetry-loving Jean-Yves. His experience with Wall Street leads him to some prescient conclusions: "[E]very last one of these guys is working some scheme... They call themselves investment bankers, traders, financial intermediaries, brokers, market makers. Unmakers is more like it."

Contemplating Matthew Arnold's poem "Dover Beach," Jean-Yves concludes that "the world is ignorant and violent but that we have one salvation before us, which is to hold tight the people we love and to be true to them." A satisfying conclusion draws it all together.

Delightful fun with a surprisingly warm heart.

—*Kirkus Reviews*

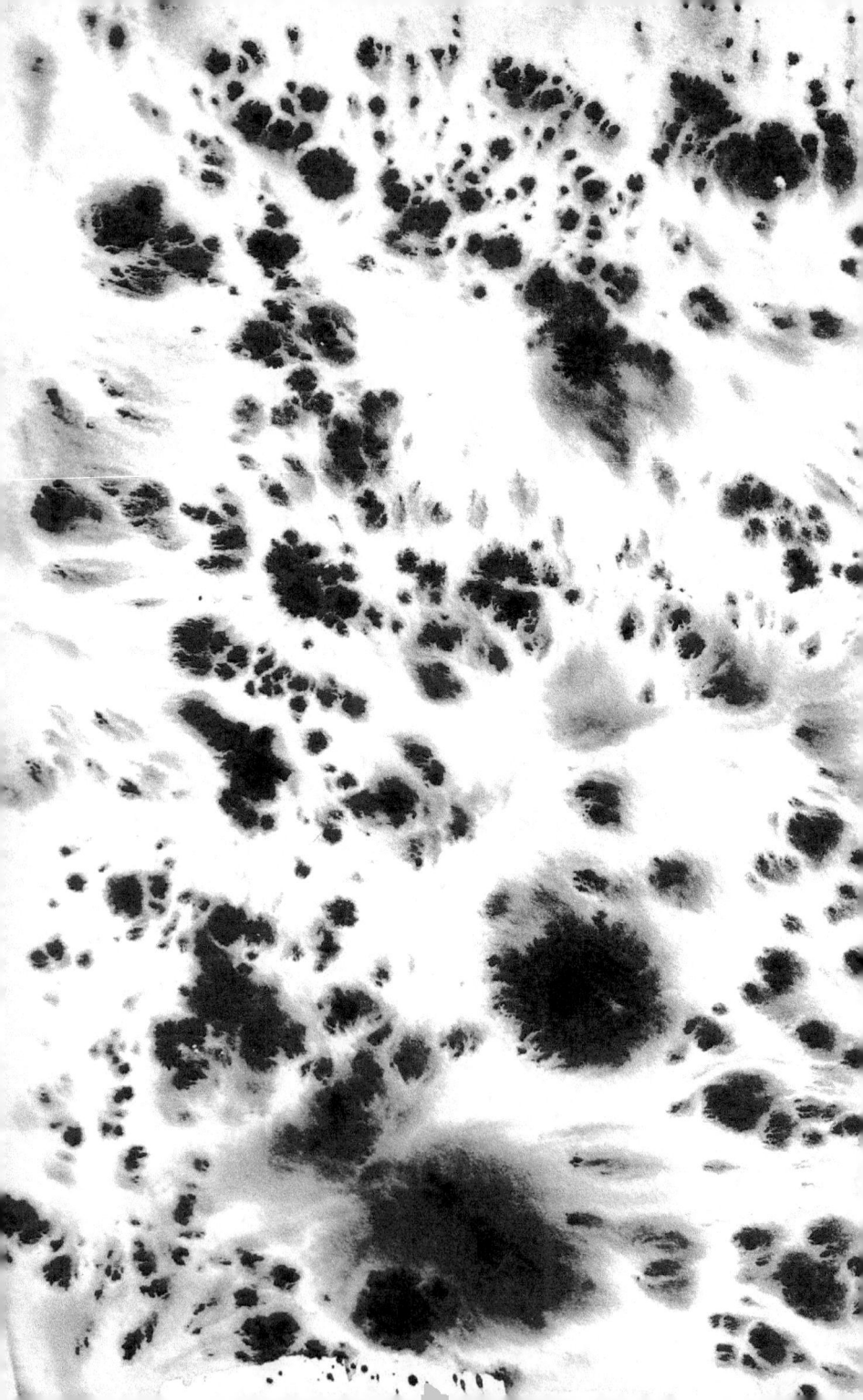

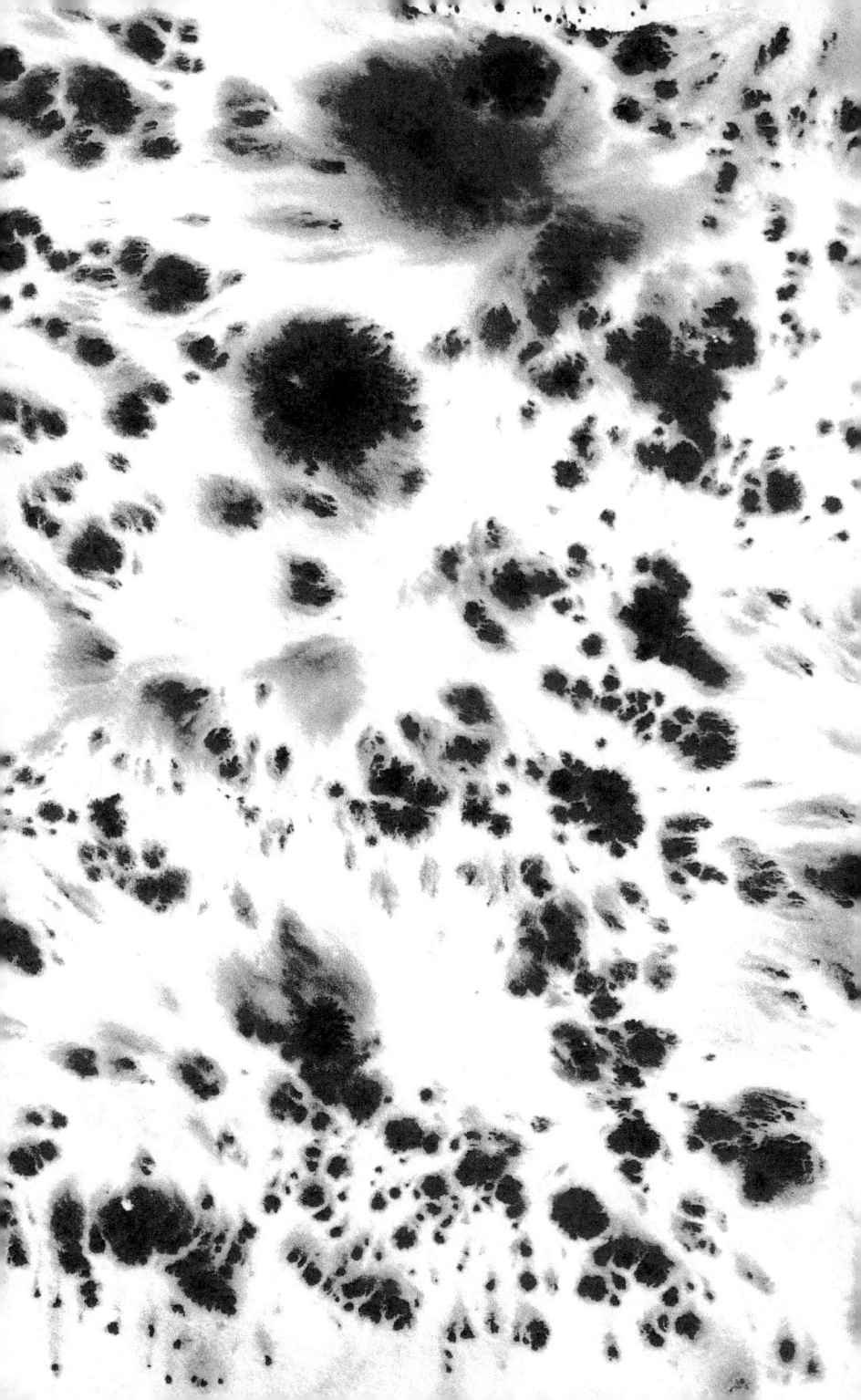